All Things Together

Mary,

Thank you for your faithful service to our Lord.

Richard L. Marshall

All Things Together

Richard Marshall

 New Harbor Press

All Things Together

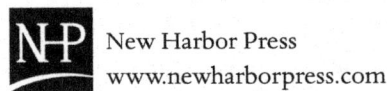 New Harbor Press
www.newharborpress.com

Copyright, © 2016 Richard L. Marshall

All rights reserved. No part of this book may be reproduced in any form, except for brief quotations in reviews, without the written permission of the author.

Printed in the United States of America. All rights reserved under International Copyright Law.

ISBN 978-1-63357-068-9

Library of Congress Control Number: TBD

All scripture quotations are taken from the American Standard Version of the Bible (ASV) (Public Domain).

DEDICATION

Second only to my Heavenly Father and my Lord and
Savior Jesus Christ, this book is dedicated to my family.
My wife Elizabeth, and our five children, John,
Martha Courtney, James, Joseph and Mary Bolen.
They have been a constant support for me,
and a continual source of strength through my ministry.
A special thanks for the completion of this book goes to my wife
and to our daughter Martha Courtney
and Linda Kolodzik and Randy
and Sherry Tilson for the
many hours they spent in proof reading.

ENDORSEMENTS

"Dick Marshall is on a short list of my favorite people. With his cheerful faith and quiet confidence, he and his wife, Betty have recognized a lifelong calling to serve troubled congregations that have exhausted others' capacity to lead. He is as one of the "others... of whom the world was not worthy" in Hebrews 11. -Michael L Chambers, PhD Chancellor & Vice Provost, Johnson University Florida

"Richard Marshall shares helpful and encouraging stories from a lifetime of ministry. His love for the Lord and for the people he serves is evident on every page. The underlying wisdom provides the young reader with principles to sustain an enduring ministry and reminds the more experienced minister of the daily delights and struggles of ministry service." -Lyle Bundy, Professor, Johnson University Florida

"Dick Marshall loves God and lives by God's rules. He is a gifted preacher, an extraordinary teacher and a loving friend with the humble heart of a servant. We can't wait to read his newest endeavor."
- Werner and Edie Koenighaus, former church Deacon and church secretary, First Christian Church, Pompano Beach, Florida

ENDORSEMENTS

"I have been privileged to know Bro. Dick Marshall and his family for many years. Years ago Bro. Marshall served as the preaching minister of the church I now serve–First Christian Church of Kissimmee, Fla. He not only laid a groundwork for solid Biblical doctrine here at FCC, but he has accomplished that task everywhere he has preached. He exemplifies the attitude and character of Christ and has been a great witness for Christ. Few men that I have known in my ministry have embodied the integrity that this man has shown to so many people for so many years. His ministry reflections within this book will be a blessing to everyone who reads them" - James C. Book, Minister

"I had the privilege for two years, while going to Bible college to sit in the pew and take in as much teaching as I could as Richard Marshall preached the Gospel. I was also blessed to sit in his classroom as he taught my first year preaching classes. Mr. Marshall, as I still call him, preached the Word boldly, but yet with such a kind and loving spirit. He has been a great mentor to me through the years since, not only as an evangelist and teacher, but also as a great Christian friend. He and his wife, Betty are both humble, faithful servants of the Lord."
- Kevin Ziegler, Evangelist, SOUTH SIDE CHURCH OF CHRIST, Danville, Illinois

CONTENTS

THE GLORY DAYS	1
THE STORM CLOUDS GATHER	15
THE STORM BREAKS	29
THE TRIAL	41
THE GOSPEL NOT BOUND	75
EVIDENCE RE-EXAMINED	97
A BRIGHTER DAY BREAKS	105
CONVICTION RECONFIRMED	125
MANY ROSES, BUT A FEW THORNS	131
THE STRUGGLES OF STEVEN	147
STEVEN'S ZEALOUS RETURN	165
THE NEW VENTURE FLOURISHES	175
COMPASSION AND COURAGE	181

CONTENTS

THE FINAL GLORY   191

END NOTES   197

FOREWORD

I have been extremely reluctant to write this book. After all Ecclesiastes 12:12 in the New American Standard Bible reads: "…..my son, be warned: the writing of many books is endless, and excessive devotion to books is wearying to the body." With so many good books available by much more capable writers than I, why should I add to the plethora of written material that surrounds us?

But there were those who kept asking me to put some of the things I had presented in sermons or Bible lessons in writing. Others, including several preacher friends and members of congregations I have served, suggested that I compile and publish some of the occasional essays and articles I had written.

Paramount among those who suggested that I write a book was Kathy Nymetz Walters. When I was ministering at Pompano Beach Christian Church in Florida in the early 1980s Kathy suggested that I write a book. Every time our paths have crossed since then, Kathy would say, "Have you written that book yet?" If there is any merit in this book, thank Kathy. Dare I also say if it bores you to death, blame her?

Because of these suggestions I had at times felt the urge to do some writing, and now that retirement years are here I can no longer use the excuse of being too busy. Still, I seldom thought I had anything really worthy of putting into print.

FOREWORD

Then in the wee hours of the morning over a year ago the thought for this book came into mind. Although still a bit reluctant, I finally decided to tell this story.

This book is fiction. However, several of the incidents in it tell the stories, under different names, of real life people and events. I have noted these by end notes, and **it is my belief that the greatest benefit from this book might come from reading these end notes.** In them the true names of the persons involved and the times and places of the events are given. I suggest that when you see a number indicating an end note, you turn immediately to the end note and to see the documentation of the real life event. I believe these events, which are given to support the proposition of the book, might provide support to those facing similar situations and difficulties in life.

My prayer is that as you read you will find encouragement in your walk with King Jesus.

THE GLORY DAYS

It would be hard to imagine a more impressive couple! The groom was a handsome, strapping man six feet, two inches tall with brown, wavy hair. The bride was absolutely stunning: a slender figure, five feet, eight inches tall, long, glistening black hair, and dark eyes that seemed to have a constant twinkle. The well proportioned features of her face, and glistening white teeth were truly radiant when she broke into the smile that seemed to come so easily for her. As she stood in her white dress with the long, flowing train, she was indeed a vision of loveliness, the epitome of a beautiful June bride.

And what potential lay before them! Just two weeks earlier Robert Morganton had received his Master of Arts degree in Christian Ministry from Clovernook Seminary. He had graduated Cum Laude. Kathleen Bailey had graduated from Clovernook Christian University, with a Bachelor of Science in Children's Ministry, and a minor in Office Procedure. She had graduated Magna Cum Laude.

They had both worked in weekend ministries, youth rallies, summer camps and various other ministries during their college years. Robert was an effective speaker and leader, and Kathleen was an excellent soloist, and during their college years the two of them had been in almost constant demand.

Just as the final semester of their college and seminary work was beginning, Kathy had said to Bob, "Honey, my father is retiring.

Why don't you see if the church at Conner's Crossing where he has been serving would be interested in you becoming their minister?" Bob had said, "Kathy, I'm reluctant to take the initiative in applying for a ministry. I believe if the Lord has a place where He wants me to serve somehow He will call me there without my having to run before Him."

This surprised Kathy, and although she admired the conviction of her husband-to-be, she was less hesitant to "run before God." She had called her father and reminded him of Bob's coming graduation, and told him of the excellent academic record Bob had compiled, and of his popularity as a speaker and Christian worker. Her father, Alan Bailey, had given Bob's name to the pulpit committee of the New Haven church where he had been serving for seventeen years, and told them of his daughter's high recommendation. Brother Bailey had served the church well, and was deeply loved and respected by the congregation, and they considered his suggestion as worthy of investigation. Therefore as a committee they had driven the seventy miles to Robert and Kathy's commencement exercises in which Robert had a part on the program. They had spoken about him with some of the faculty and administrators of the college, and all of them had made positive comments about Robert. Being favorably impressed in these conversations, the committee invited Robert to come and meet with the elders for an interview, and if they were in agreement that he might be the man for the ministry there, they would ask him to preach to the congregation as the one they recommended to succeed Brother Bailey as their preacher. By a vote of 132 to 3, the congregation voted to extend the call to Robert Morganton to be their preaching minister. Although Bob had felt that Kathy had perhaps been a bit guilty of "running before God," he had to consider the strong vote of the congregation to truly be the call of God. His ministry began the 3rd Sunday in June, just after Bob and Kathy's wedding and honeymoon.

Kathy suggested that she and Bob move in with her father. He had used the housing allowance which the church had given him from the beginning of his ministry to purchase a home rather than just rent. It had been on a twenty year mortgage, and having preached there for seventeen years, there were only three years left on the mortgage. Kathy said that since her mother had died, and her two brothers had moved away, and her younger sister, Karen, was in college, her dad was alone and lonely in a big house. Bob, who would now begin to receive the housing allowance could pay the rest of the mortgage and then make payments to Kathy's father for the equity he had built up in the house. It sounded like a win-win situation, and Bob readily agreed.

The ministry went well. Alan Bailey had done well with the church. They were united, they were firm in their faith, they loved God, they loved each other, and they loved their community. There were three elders: John Black, Clarence White and Roger Jones, who was the chairman of the group. They used to joke saying no one could accuse them of racism, with both Black and White in the church leadership.

And indeed they could not be accused of racism. There were two black families and three Latino families in the membership. Herman and Inga Steadman had come from Germany, and both still spoke with a German accent. Yet the harmony within the church family was exemplary. Color or national origin made no difference in the operation or participation in any of the church functions.

In one of the weekend ministries in which Bob had served during his college days there had been the practice one Sunday evening each month of the folk sharing testimonies. Sometimes this would just be reciting a passage of the person's favorite Scripture. Bob soon learned that each month Mrs. Anderson, in her late seventies, would say "My favorite verse of Scripture is Romans 8:28 - "We know that God causes all things to work together for good to those who love Him, to those who are called according to His purpose." The genuine faith of Mrs. Anderson, the sincerity with which she quoted the verse, plus that wonderful promise of the verse made this become Bob's favorite Scripture also. In fact, this verse, along with Philippians 4:6,7 "Be anxious for nothing, but in everything by prayer and supplication, with thanksgiving, let your requests be made known to God, and the peace of God which surpasses all comprehension shall guard your hearts and your minds in Christ Jesus," became the theme of Bob's preaching ministry.

Bob's sermons were always thoughtful and well prepared. He preached with transparency and fervor. While Bob did not memorize his sermons, he did memorize the major Biblical texts he would use, and he carefully constructed his outlines so that the things he had prepared would come easily to his memory as he preached. Thus, even though he preached without notes his messages were not disjointed or rambling. His messages resonated well with the congregation, and it wasn't long till the people began to comment to their neighbors and friends about their excellent preacher. The church was growing nicely. When he began his ministry in June, the congregation averaged 175 in attendance. At the end of the year they were approaching 200, and sometimes went 2 or 3 over that mark.

Bob not only preached well, he also enjoyed personal evangelism. Consequently people responding to the invitation and accepting Christ became more and more frequent. Seeing folk being immersed into Christ each Lord's Day became more the usual event than the exceptional. Bob had often taken other men in the congregation with him when he made his teaching calls, and it wasn't unusual for one of them to call him during the week and tell of someone they had taught who now wanted to be baptized into Christ.

Kathy also proved to be an invaluable asset to Bob's ministry. Her beautiful voice and frequent solos added much to their worship experience. She prayed for Bob, and with Bob, and gave him absolutely unrestricted support in his ministry.

The calls from area churches for Bob to come and speak to them began to come rapidly. He developed a three message series from Romans 8:28. The first message, "God Causes all Things to Work Together for Good" emphasized that God was still at work in His world. What some might call accidental, or incidental, or coincidental were in reality providential. Some might even call them miraculous but Bob hesitated to use that term when the things being worked out did not involve God intervening in natural law or the setting aside of natural law, but rather God's orchestrating natural things and events for the benefit of His children. He told the story of a man who had had surgery for ulcers which caused the removal of two thirds of his stomach. The surgery had gone well, but a few days later gangrene developed. Quite late one night the doctor called from the hospital and told the wife that the situation with her husband had become so critical that it was going to be necessary to perform surgery again, go into the stomach and remove the gangrene. He asked her to come immediately to the hospital to make a critical decision. Dr. Henry's judgment was that her husband was not strong enough to survive surgery, but that if it were not performed, he believed that the gangrene would kill her husband before morning. It seemed a no win situation.

The wife called her preacher to meet her and her son at the hospital. When he got there, preparations were already being made for the surgery. It was asked if there was a room where the family and the preacher could have privacy for prayer. Someone in the room said that the adjacent patient room was vacant and could be used. The preacher, the patient's wife and son went into that room, shut the door and prayed as the surgical preparations continued. Some moments later, when they came out Dr. Henry met them in the hall. He said "While you were in there, Dr. Keene came into the hospital. I hadn't seen him in 8 years, but when I did, it reminded me that 8 years ago Dr. Keene had a very similar medical case with one of his patients. I told him of the situation with your husband and he told me that he had flooded his patient with a particular chemical treatment, and it had reversed the development of the gangrene. I suggest we try his treatment rather than the surgery."

The wife and son agreed to that. There was nothing more the family or preacher could do, so at the doctor's suggestion they left to go home and get some rest. The next day when the preacher went back to the hospital, the patient was sitting up in bed, energetically talking with others in the room. In a short time he was fully recovered, and went home again. Certainly, Bob contended, such precise timing could be explained only by the providence of God. (1)

A second illustration Bob used was that of Denton Milford. Denton had previously had brain surgery for a malady that had caused frequent blackouts and had made it impossible for him to work. Those surgeries had been successful, but now, at age 52, Denton had an even more life threatening ailment; a blood clot in his lung that had become so critical that the only hope to save his life was a very high risk surgical procedure. In the hospital in Orlando, Florida he was told that the only person they knew of who had successfully performed the needed surgery was Dr. Nate Kyle, in

California. Denton was given the option of being flown by helicopter to California or having the surgery done by a local team in Orlando.

Denton had been well treated by the staff in Orlando, and he had come to know them, and they him, on a personal basis. If he were to have the surgery in Orlando, Dr. Shawn Schwinn-Calvert would do it. Dr. Benjamin, Denton's cardiologist, said that if there was any surgeon who could do the job, it was Dr. Schwinn-Calvert. Dr. Benjamin, and a pulmonary hypertension specialist, Dr. Andrew Palmer, and a very capable nurse practitioner, Cindy Pawlkas, would complete Dr. Schwinn-Calvert's surgical team.

The team from Orlando had been in conference with Dr. Kyle in California. While the surgery was in progress, by modern technology, Dr. Kyle would be watching in California, and available for advice if needed. The flight to California would be risky in itself, and the expense would greatly add to the cost which Denton and his family were already wondering how they could possibly pay. They opted to have the Orlando, Florida team perform the surgery. The surgery took nearly the entire day. Some time after the initial surgery had ended, Dr. Palmer took another look at what the post-op pictures had shown, and was disturbed. While the clot that had been removed was nearly the size of a golf ball, Dr. Palmer detected other smaller clots which he said must also be removed. These he said could also be life threatening. So that evening Denton was opened again, and the other clots removed.

When the second operation was over, Denton was hooked to an array of tubes and wires. As he lay there that evening barely breathing Dr. Palmer said: "He's got a one chance in a hundred of surviving through the night. All we can do now is pray."

And pray they did, with an urgency and fervency few ever experience.

And God answered their prayer. It was 4 or 5 days before Denton became fully cognizant, but as he was recovering his doctors commented, "We have made medical history." This was another incident that preacher Bob said was beyond the ordinary, and an illustration of the expertise of men and women who acknowledged their dependence upon God being blessed by His marvelous providence. (2)

The second message in Bob's series was that these assurances are to those "who love God." He stressed that God loves us abundantly, that, according to Romans 5:5, by His Spirit He pours out His love into our hearts. He stated that he believed that God did this not only for the benefit of the believer, but so that His love might overflow from the heart of the believer to a hurting world.

The third message, "Those Called According to His Purpose," challenged the hearers to realize that God has a purpose for each life, and that the believers' lives find fullness and contentment only as they brought their wills into conformity to God's will to fulfill that purpose.

This series found a hungry audience, and the invitations to speak at churches throughout the area became so numerous that Bob had to reluctantly decline some of them to give proper attention to his local ministry.

And that ministry continued to prosper. There was peace and happiness in the local congregation. Preacher Bob and the congregation were held in high regard by all the community. Bob and his father-in-law had a great relationship. Bob greatly appreciated Alan's advice, counsel and encouragement, and Alan admired the energy, imagination and faithfulness of his son-in-law. Bob thanked Kathy for first suggesting they come to this ministry, and thanked God daily for the joy in service they were experiencing.

The household grew a bit the following May when Kathy's younger sister, Karen, graduated from nursing school. The family still did not fill the huge two story house in which they lived, so Karen moved back home to make her residence with her father, her sister and her brother-in-law.

Karen was a delightful addition to the family, and to the church. She was a petite girl, 5 foot and 1 inch tall. She had auburn hair and eyes of a vivid green color. Like Kathy, she had lovely facial features. She had a bubbling personality. She laughed easily and sometimes had a tendency to giggle, which might have been irritating, if it hadn't been so charming. While Kathy had a great solo voice, Karen had a very mellow alto which not only enhanced congregational singing, but blended beautifully with Kathy when they sang oft-requested duets in their worship services.

Bob was strong on developing church leadership and had started a class in the church for just that purpose. In addition to that, he regularly met one on one with men in whom he saw a potential for leadership. One of these was Jerry Johnson. Jerry was a jovial fellow who had become a Christian about six years earlier, and was active in and supportive of all the church programs. Most of the congregation called him J.J. He was well liked by all the congregation, but probably it was his jovial nature that had kept him from being selected for leadership earlier. He had a quick wit and a sharp sense of humor and was a bit of a practical joker at times. It may have been the fun-loving side of his nature that made folk fail to see his spiritual depth. As Bob worked with him, and as the elders conferred with him, they came to appreciate his Biblical knowledge, his compassion, and genuine love for the kingdom of God. He was recommended to the congregation and elected to the eldership. He proved to be a valuable addition to the church leadership with a down to earth wisdom and practical suggestions when the elders found it necessary to confront problems in the church family.

The elders meetings were a pleasant experience for Bob. Every other month they met in the church office on a Tuesday evening. Their agenda was simple; they discussed the spiritual needs of the congregation and shared their thoughts on how to deal with them. They did not vote, but continued to discuss each matter until they came to a consensus. Then they prayed together. They spent little time with material matters as they had entrusted most of these to the deacons. Usually their evening meetings were over in about an hour.

On the alternate months their meetings were different, and longer. These meetings were held in the morning at Barton's Pharmacy and Cafe'. Two of the men were retired, but Jerry Johnson had to leave his real estate office and Roger Jones was able to leave his work as Director of the city Department of Parks and Recreation for the meetings. Preacher Bob and the four elders ate breakfast together and in this casual setting took plenty of time to discuss some matters concerning the church, but more often they discussed how the church might impact the community more effectively. By the time the morning breakfast patrons had left their tables the corner of the cafe was pretty isolated. If sensitive matters came up, they of course dismissed those until a more private time. The men sometimes spent 3 hours in these meetings, but when the lunch crowd started to arrive, they would end their discussion to make room for the patrons.

Bonnie Barton who owned and managed the cafe' had offered to place a moveable partition to separate their table from the rest of the patrons, but the men preferred to leave it open. The people of the community soon became aware that they met there regularly, and felt free to come up and talk with the men. This of course slowed down the progress of their meetings, but it afforded invaluable opportunities for contacts with people in the community that never would have developed within the walls of their building. It made them more aware of how they could more effectively be the "salt of the earth."

And the church was having a "salty" influence. They had become the conscience of the community. Bob had not been timid about taking a stand on moral issues, and the high moral concepts of the congregation had their impact. When a gambling concern wanted to bring a casino into the county, Bob had preached against the moral dangers of gambling. He and several of the congregation had gone before the county commissioners to oppose the casino. When it was put to a vote, the county overwhelmingly opposed the casino, and it never did come into the county. The local weekly newspaper had taken a stand against the casino, and in print had lauded Bob and the church for their effective part in preventing the casino from coming.

Bonnie Barton was one of the best known and highly respected members of the community. Conner's Crossing was a small town in an agricultural part of the state. It originally was only a few houses and a small general store located where two state highways intersected. The building of a vegetable processing plant and a small concrete plant had "swelled" the population to about 2400 people. Nearly all of these had known Bonnie most of her life. Her given name was Bonita, and shortly after she married "Buddy" Barton they had opened the Pharmacy with the small cafe' in it. They had a son whom the town knew as "Little Buddy." When the boy was 4 years old, his father died, and Bonnie had been working hard for the last three years to keep the business going. The challenges had been great, and those who knew Bonnie best saw the evidences of the stress she faced in her life. She was a woman of most pleasant appearance, but most of the time looked tired. However, at the cafe' she was always bright and cheerful. She had ash blond hair and light blue eyes, which unfortunately were often subdued by the tired look that surrounded them. Yet her upbeat manner, and her cheery greeting to all who entered the cafe' endeared her to everyone. Because of the need to keep operating costs low, she worked the cash register and also helped serve her customers. She seemed to genuinely appreciate the fact that the men of the church met there regularly.

Thursday was Bob's day off, and although it sometimes had to be forfeited when serious illness of a member or a similar emergency came up, on most Thursdays Bob played golf. The usual foursome was Bob, his father in law, Alan, the chairman of the elders, Roger Jones, and Denver Newton, the minister of the Hillsborough church eighteen miles away. This was a refreshing time for all them. Their scores were usually from the high eighties to the high nineties, so no one could accuse them of deserting their church work to play too much golf. Just for fun they began to challenge each other by playing for a penny a hole. If one of them won a hole, they got a penny from each of the other three. There was no payment made if the holes were tied. This way if someone lost every hole he would only lose fifty four cents, and if he won every hole his winning would similarly be only fifty four cents for the day. When they finished their eighteen holes they would go into the lobby, drink cokes and "divvy up" their penny per hole winnings or losses. This was accompanied by a good bit of razzing and laughter. Most often it was preacher Newton who claimed the most of the winnings.

When Father's Day came just a year after preacher Bob had begun his ministry at the New Haven church, preacher Bob was at his best. He confessed at the beginning that he could not preach this message claiming the advantage of experience, but only with the confidence that he had from God because of His instructions to fathers from the pen of the apostle Paul. He presented an excellent exegetical message from Ephesians 6:1-4. He dealt with the heavy responsibilities of parenthood, and then with it's joys and blessings. He referred to Psalms 127:3-5a: "Sons are a heritage from the Lord, children a reward from Him. Like arrows in the hands of a warrior are sons born in one's youth. Blessed is the man whose quiver is full of them." He described how from the time of their engagement he and Kathy had planned to have a large family, so while he was not preaching from experience, he was preaching with an excited anticipation. Then the congregation could discern his ecstasy, as he announced that Kathy was pregnant, and they were joyously looking forward to being parents of the first, but certainly what they hoped would be far from their last, child.

Bob's joy was almost impossible to contain. He could hardly believe how good God had been to them and how He continued to pour blessings upon them far beyond their fondest expectations. He was serving a church he loved dearly, and who loved and supported him, the Lord was blessing the church with exciting growth, he had a beautiful and supportive wife, he was about to experience what he had always looked forward to as one of life's richest blessings as he became a father.

But things were about to change!

THE STORM CLOUDS GATHER

Kathy was radiant in her pregnancy. Her complexion had a glow, and her eyes seemed to have an even brighter than usual twinkle. Her always ready smile was now almost constant. She wore maternity clothes with an obvious pride. Daily Bob and Kathy thanked God for the fullness of life and the anticipated joy of parenthood.

But at the beginning of her eighth month of pregnancy the heartache came. Late one afternoon Kathy suddenly experienced a strange and very severe pain. Bob rushed her to the Conner's Crossing Medical Clinic, and she was hurriedly taken to a room. Dr. Marvin Moreland, who had been Bob and Kathy's doctor for about two years now, immediately began an examination. Bob was a little surprised when Dr. Moreland asked him to leave the room.

The Medical Clinic was really a small hospital. It had only eight patient rooms, but each room had two beds, so they could handle sixteen patients. This seemed adequate for their small community. Although the clinic was small, the Conner's Crossing people were proud of the excellent care they received there, and the high quality and expertise of the doctors and staff.

Bob was ushered to the surgical waiting room where he waited in tormented anxiety for what seemed an eternity. Then Dr. Moreland appeared at the door, with an extremely dismayed look on his face. Although Bob was rising from his chair to meet him, Dr. Moreland motioned to Bob to stay seated. He walked across the room, took a seat beside Bob, and placed his arm around his shoulders. "Bob," he said, "This is not good. I have no idea what happened because when I saw Kathy two weeks ago she and the baby were in excellent shape. However, the baby has for some unknown reason died in the womb, and a raging infection, some kind of aggressive toxic infection, has invaded Kathy's body. We are going to have to do radical surgery, and we must do it immediately. The operating room is being prepared now, and my assistant and my best surgical nurse are right now scrubbing up for surgery. This is going to be a big operation, and a dangerous operation. I know you're going to be praying, but right now would you also pray for me. You know I'll do my best, but I must tell you, this kind of surgery often has serious complications."

With arms around each other's shoulders, the preacher and the good doctor prayed together.

The next three hours were agony for Bob. He alternately prayed and wept. He prayed, "Lord, your word tells me that if I pray and make supplication I need not be anxious, and that you will give me a peace beyond my comprehension. Father, I'm heartbroken, I plead with you for my wife, but still, I confess, I am overwhelmed with anxiety. I cannot understand why this child that Kathy and I already loved so dearly, and so much wanted to raise to love and honor and serve you has been taken from us. I believe your word, Father, and I beg for understanding, and for the peace you promised. God, please spare Kathy's life, please bless Dr. Moreland, and please be with us through this sorrow, and grant us your peace."

However, in the hour of that crushing sorrow, Bob could find no peace.

Finally Dr. Moreland came back into the room. His expression let Bob know immediately that all was not good. Again, he came to Bob and placed an arm around his shoulder. "Bob" he said with pathos, "Kathy came through the surgery fine. Physically, she will be all right. However, she will not be able to bear children." Bob prayed, "Thank you Lord for sparing my wife." Then he wept openly and unashamedly.

"I must tell you something else, Bob," said Dr. Moreland. "Kathy will be going through some significant hormonal changes as a result of this surgery. You need to be prepared for some behavioral, even personality changes, in Kathy."

Bob said "Thank you doctor. I am deeply thankful that Kathy is alive, and with the help of the Lord I can deal with behavioral changes. It's hard to understand it now, but you know, doctor, I have often preached God works all things for the good of His children, and somehow, I believe that in His ultimate plan He will in time bring that about, even through this heartbreak, and that some day in some way Kathy and I will find that peace that is beyond our understanding."

It was some weeks before Kathy was able to attend church again. During that time the congregation heard an obviously heartbroken preacher. Yet through his heartbreak he preached with a sympathetic heart that brought hope and encouragement to many hurting people. He had an obvious empathy that he had not had before. The church continued to grow, and now was regularly running over 300 in attendance.

The congregation surrounded Bob and Kathy with their love. While his relationship with the people had always been good, he now felt a warm fellowship beyond anything he had previously experienced. Several ladies of the congregation came quite regularly to visit Kathy. Often husbands and wives came together. They would bring food, or small gifts or cards; all expressions of love for their preacher and his wife. This, he knew, was the deep fellowship of the spirit, a fellowship and unity unmatched by anything in the world.

The day came when Kathy was again able to come to the meetings of the congregation. When she first stepped into the building the congregation applauded, then cheered. The eyes of both Bob and Kathy filled with tears of appreciation and joy. As peace once again flooded his soul, Bob prayed, "Thank you Father, your promise indeed is true."

But, in spite of the wise warnings by Dr. Moreland, Bob was not prepared for what was happening in the life of Kathy.

There were behavioral changes in Kathy far more than Bob or even Dr. Moreland anticipated. She lost her appetite, and food was distasteful for her. She began to lose weight. The spring in her step was gone, and she now shuffled along, almost dragging her feet. Her once regal posture changed, and rather than the erect and confident poise she once had, she slumped forward, and over time became a bit stoop shouldered. These changes took place slowly, but over time were most noticeable. As her weight loss continued, her clothes now hung on her as if on a skeleton. The sparkle in her eyes was gone, and her cheeks were hollow. Much of the time her once beautiful, shining hair looked unkempt. Her deep depression, in spite of the medication Dr. Moreland had prescribed, became obvious to all.

However, Kathy mustered all her strength to fight this. She and Bob prayed daily for her to improve. When they went out in public Kathy, who had worn makeup only sparsely before, tried to bring back the earlier glow in her complexion with more makeup, often to extremes. In the church meetings, Kathy struggled to make the best appearance she could. Her smile, once so winsome, now was obviously forced. Sometimes she would smile and laugh when with people, but when she returned home she was often short-tempered, and in frustration would often lash out at Bob.

Yet, she seemed to draw closer to her father. She had always loved him deeply, but now seemed to lean more and more heavily upon him. Bob sometimes felt excluded when Kathy would pour her heart out to her father more than to her husband. Kathy seemed to have lost her confidence that Bob still loved her. The realization that she could never give Bob the children she knew he so fervently desired deepened her depression, which, even though several medications were tried, seemed to grow worse.

Nevertheless there were times when she would "snap out of it" for a while. At such times she would laugh again, and occasionally almost become giddy. This dual personality concerned Bob greatly, for after the periods of seeming happiness, she would sink into an even deeper depression. Yet Bob admired the efforts Kathy was making. She did maintain a vital faith in God, and realized He was the only hope she had for a brighter future.

Bob regularly told her that he loved her deeply. He quoted the words of Elkanah to Hannah when Hannah was grieving because she had not had children, "why do you weep and why do you not eat and why is your heart sad? Am I not better to you than ten sons?"(3) She retorted by saying, "But Bob does not Malachi say in the second chapter of his book that the reason for marriage and fidelity in marriage is to raise up godly offspring?(4) Yet I am not able to do that with and for you. What purpose then is there for me to live?"

Bob was finding it hard to sleep. Kathy, however, was always sleepy, and some nights would fall asleep on the couch in the living room. Rather than wake her, Bob would pull a light blanket which they kept on the back of the couch over her and go to bed alone. To help himself fall asleep, Bob would rehearse in his mind passages of Scripture he had memorized. These included Psalms 1 and 23, portions of the sermon on the mount, the 12th chapter of Romans, the 13th chapter of I Corinthians, the 3rd chapter of Philippians and other passages. During these days he found himself doing that many nights.

Through these difficult days, Bob kept reminding himself that in time all this would work out for good. However, things were soon to get even harder.

Leonardo was the family pet, and a great dog he was. He was a Labrador/Golden Retriever mix, a huge dog, but loving and gentle. He was well trained, and without a leash walked on the right side of those who would take him for a walk. Leonardo loved these walks, and Alan, Bob's father-in-law, would take him for a walk almost every evening, usually just before the family sat down for supper. One evening Alan and Leonardo had gone for their walk. Bob, Kathy and Karen were just about ready for the evening meal when suddenly they heard Leonardo barking and scratching at the front door. They went to the door, and Leonardo barked at them, and then turned to run down the porch steps. When they did not follow him, he came back, barked loudly at them, and again ran down the steps. They immediately realized he was trying to get them to follow him, and a sudden uneasy feeling came upon them. They followed him and when they got to the sidewalk they saw two cars pulled off the side of the road about two hundred yards from the house. Anticipating what had happened, they ran with Leonardo toward where the cars were stopped. They saw Alan lying prostrate across the sidewalk. Two men and a woman were there, one of the men bending over the body of Alan and the other man and woman looking on with deep concern. The woman pulled a phone from her purse and called 911.

THE STORM CLOUDS GATHER

When the medics arrived, they could detect no breathing or pulse. Kathy and Karen burst into tears. The medics attempted CPR. At the hospital it was confirmed what the medics had suspected, Alan had apparently died instantly. He had suffered a brain aneurism.

The daughters took the death very hard. Karen could not stop crying, but Kathy's tears were less profuse. She seemed to almost be in denial that her father had died. She talked hardly at all, and withdrew even deeper into the shell with which she had surrounded herself at the loss of her unborn child.

Kathy's two older brothers returned for the funeral. They, along with their sisters, each had a word of testimony at the services. Bob also expressed his admiration of his father-in-law, and told of what a great support and encouragement he had been to him in the ministry of the New Haven church. Bob's good friend, Denver Newton who had been a part of the foursome including Alan, with whom he played golf, came from the Hillsborough church to preach the funeral message. He had a most comforting message from Revelation 14:13 "Blessed are the dead who die in the Lord from now on! Yes, says the Spirit, that they may rest from their labors, for their deeds follow with them."

At the graveside, after all but the family had left, Kathy went to stand for a few moments by the casket before it was lowered into the grave. Bob stepped up beside her, and then Karen came and stood on the other side of Bob. Bob slipped his arm around his softly sobbing wife. Then Karen burst into uncontrolled weeping again, threw her arms around Bob, and laid her head against his chest. Bob embraced her for a moment, and then felt a surge of mixed emotions like nothing he had ever experienced. At Karen's embrace he felt a surge of pleasure which he had not known for months, but this was immediately dispelled by an overpowering feeling of guilt. He knew that Karen's act had been in a moment of deep grief, and a grasping for comfort, but he felt shame because of the feeling of pleasure it gave him. He quickly broke from her embrace, and the three of them walked to the funeral car awaiting them, and left the cemetery.

A large part of Kathy had died with the loss of her child, and now with the loss of her father another part of her died. She was inconsolable, and her despondency grew even deeper. Dr. Moreland recommended a professional counselor, and although it was a cost hard for Kathy and Bob to assume, she did go for regular counseling. Bob attended some of the sessions with her, but the counselor also saw Kathy alone many times. After the third session the counselor had said to Bob: "She is one of the most severe cases of depression I have ever seen. This will take a long time, and you will have to be extremely understanding and patient with her." Bob vowed he would, and Kathy's recovery became his primary concern in life, and the subject of his daily prayers.

There were brief episodes, where it seemed progress was being made, but these were followed by periods of despondency that seemed to grow longer and longer. Kathy would swing from times of sullen withdrawal to periods of irritation and aggression. She knew Bob was trying his best, and would apologize for her behavior, but soon would become irritated at some insignificant thing and lash out at him. Sometimes these attacks were vicious and cruel. She often told him he was not nearly the preacher her father had been, and would tell him her father could have handled a church situation much better than he did. Then she would turn and hug him, and ask again for his forgiveness. Bob began to wonder if she was feeling personal guilt because of the fact that she could not bear children, and that she maybe even thought that her attitudes had contributed to the death of her father.

Both those in the community and in the church tried to help. Because she opened her cafe' Sundays, Bonnie Barton did not attend church. However she knew of the situation at the Morganton house, and one day after the meeting of Bob with the elders at the cafe' she asked Bob who did the cooking at home? He said that when Alan was still alive, he did most of it with Kathy's help. Partly due to her own distaste, almost aversion, to food, Kathy now found it unpleasant, even difficult for her to do any cooking. He told Bonnie that he usually got his own breakfast, and two or three times, sometimes even four times a week he had lunch at the cafeteria of the medical center where Karen worked. He would schedule his calls at the hospital near the noon hour, and met Karen for lunch.

Bonnie said, "I have a proposal I'd like you to think about. On week days I come down here to get things ready for the breakfast crowd. Although we do not open until 7 o'clock I come at about 5:30. My son, Little Buddy, leaves for school at 7:15. I don't want to get him up at 5:30, and can't get away from here just at opening time, but with school about to start I've got to figure out a way to get him to school. If I left you a key to my house, I could set the alarm for him at about 6:15, he can get up and get himself ready for school, and if you could come by and take him to school, and then come here, your breakfast would be on the house." Bob knew of the difficult time it was for Bonnie to take care of her child and her business. It sounded like a workable plan to him. Bonnie then said, "Little Buddy will only be alone for about an hour, and the door will be locked until you come and get him. At mid-afternoon when its a bit quieter here, I or one of my employees could get away to take him home from school. At closing time I always have food here that I have to dispose of, I could put together food that would be perfectly good to be warmed and used the next day, and if it's not too late at about 9:30

to 10 o'clock I could bring it by for you and Kathy and Karen to eat whenever you wanted."

Bob said "That would be a real blessing to us, and I know Kathy will really appreciate it." Karen works at the medical center from 10:00 AM. until 6:00 PM, so helping with the meals has not been easy for her. What you suggest would be a real help to all of us."

Even though Kathy continued in her therapy sessions, the bipolar tendencies increased. Sometimes she was a delight; other times she was critical and harsh. Bob appreciated the valiant effort she was making, and tried to be as understanding and sympathetic as he could. Yet, he found his own patience being stretched, and at times his irritation would show. If he responded harshly to Kathy's criticism, Kathy would break into tears, and Bob would embrace her, apologize and say, "I'm sorry Kathy, I know the struggle you're going through and I'm trying to be patient. I do love you and ask for God's strength so that both of us can get through these tough days."

Kathy still wanted to serve the Lord. Bob suggested to the elders that Kathy be given a small stipend to help him with church office work for just a few hours a week. The elders readily agreed since the church was growing, had no office help, Kathy was qualified for the work, and everyone felt it would be a measure to help Kathy regain a sense of purpose. This proved to be a wise choice - for a time.

However when the times of depression came upon Kathy, most everything that Bob did, or asked her to do, irritated her. Sometimes when disagreements came about some office procedure she would withdraw and sulk; other times she lashed out in anger. One thing Bob did was dictate letters to a recording machine, and at a time she would choose, Kathy would type these letters, bring them to Bob, and he would proof read, sign, and mail them. One day she brought in such a letter, and she had typed the phrase "hopen prayer." Bob said, "Honey, we'll have to correct the letter. Look what you have typed here. "Hopen prayer." She said "Bob, that's exactly what you said." "No honey," he replied. "I said hope and prayer. This statement makes no sense. We'll have to correct it and reprint it."

Kathy flew into a rage. "I'm not doing it" she said. "People will know what you mean as it is. If you expect me to type these letters you're going to have to speak to that machine more precisely."

"Come on Kathy," Bob said. "It's no big deal to correct it; it would only take a couple of minutes."

"No way," Kathy shot back. "I'm tired of this job anyway. You're just too hard to please."

Kathy stormed out of the office, and out of the building, and went home.

When the elders heard of the situation, they asked Bob how beneficial it had been to have office help. Bob said he had found it extremely helpful, and had freed up a good bit of time for him to spend on other aspects of the ministry.

They said, "Well, our finances are stronger than they were before, and we believe that we can afford to pay a small amount for office help. Bob, why don't you look around and see if there's someone we could find who would be able to work a few hours a week. We can't pay a salary like a business office would pay, but there may be someone who would appreciate the opportunity to work on a flexible hourly basis for a limited salary." Bob said, "I believe that would work. Let me inquire around about it."

Karen was aware of the situation, and went to the elders to volunteer her services without any salary. She said "My hours at the medical center do not start until 10:A.M. and I could easily give a couple of hours each morning to the work Kathy was doing." When this was mentioned to Bob, he agreed that would take care of the need, but stated that if anyone except his wife took the job his study door and the office door should be open at all times and the entrance to the church building should be unlocked. This didn't seem to concern them as they all knew Karen, she was Bob's sister-in-law, and they felt nothing inappropriate would take place. However the policy was set that any time Karen and Bob were in the building together, all doors inside the building would be open, and the church building itself would be unlocked.

It was soon discovered that it only took about an hour or so a day to do the things Kathy had been doing, so Karen would come in around 8:30 or 9:00 AM, bring Bob a cup of coffee from the church kitchen, check with him for any tasks that needed to be done, and leave a few minutes before 10 to get to the medical center. This was working well.

One morning she came in, put Bob's coffee on his desk, and asked if there were anything she could do. He, pointing to a particular volume said, "Karen, would you bring me that large commentary on the second shelf from the top of that bookcase?" Bob had a single step stool at the foot of the bookcase, so he could reach books on the top shelf. Karen reached for the commentary he mentioned, but with her five foot one stature, realized she couldn't reach it. She slid the step stool into place. and as she was stepping onto it, Bob realized it was a stretch for her and said, "I'm sorry Karen, I didn't realize you wouldn't be able to reach that." He got up from his chair, walked around his desk and started toward the bookshelf. As she stepped down, Karen turned her ankle and began to fall forward. Bob hurried to her, and caught her before she fell all the way. Her body fell into his, and as he lifted her up, their faces brushed together. Again Bob felt that overwhelming combination of emotion he had felt when Karen embraced him at her father's funeral. There was the undeniable pleasure he found from her nearness, but also the surge of shame. The guilt was not because he had caught her, for that was purely accidental, but because of the undeniable and, he believed, illicit pleasure he found as his arms embraced her. They quickly separated, and from the open doorway heard, "Well, I never thought I would see such a thing in this building." Mrs. Ellen Bridgewell had just come into the building to get light refreshments ready for a ladies group who met on Tuesday mornings for tea and Bible study. Bob and Karen, blushing and embarrassed, tried to explain, but Mrs. Bridgewell was obviously unconvinced.

Mrs. Bridgewell's husband had deserted her some years ago. and had married another woman. Mrs. Bridgewell was a strong believer and a faithful member of the church and had worked off her frustration and heartbreak and loneliness by throwing herself even more energetically into the work of the church. There was hardly a program of the church in which she was not actively involved. Knowing the heartache Kathy had experienced, and the difficult times she was going through, she had become very supportive of and very close to Kathy.

The rumors began.

THE STORM BREAKS

Attendance began to decline at the church. The undercurrent of suspicion obviously engendered by the rumors eroded the enthusiasm of the congregation. However, Kathy seemed to be oblivious to them. Perhaps to shield her from hurt feelings the people were careful not to mention it in her presence, or perhaps she had heard some of it but dismissed it as unfounded. At any rate, she seemed unaffected by it.

The elders soon became aware of the rumors and called a meeting to talk with Bob about it. He explained what had happened, and the confidence the men had developed in Bob, and his history of complete integrity made them immediately accept his explanation. They expressed their support of him, but suggested that it might be best if Karen stopped her volunteer work with him, and ceased coming in to lend a hand. Karen completely understood, and her volunteer work stopped. On the other hand, this may have done more harm than good, because some of the people seemed to take this as an admission of guilt.

At about this time a national church planting organization started a new congregation just six miles from the New Haven church. With the growth the New Haven congregation had previously been experiencing, they had discussed expansion, including the erection of a multipurpose building so they could offer more family life programs

THE STORM BREAKS

to the community. But with the recent decline in attendance and no staff help for the preacher they had to defer those plans. The new mega-church did have all these facilities and programs. They hired a full staff, including paid professional musicians, qualified counselors and state of the art audio and visual equipment and operators. New Haven, as well as other churches in the community, saw their members leaving to become involved in this "full service church."

Meanwhile, Bob got a phone call that rather surprised him and did lift his spirit. The Rockview church about a hundred miles away asked him to come and conduct a two session seminar on a Saturday evening and preach on Sunday morning. He mentioned his amazement that they had called him, and told them that the attendance of the church where he was serving was experiencing decline, and wondered why they had chosen him to conduct a seminar. They said they were aware that there had been some decrease in their attendance, but that it had not been as large a loss as most of the churches in the Conner's Crossing had experienced since the opening of the mega-church in the area. They also knew of the excellent work he had done from the time he had begun his ministry, and of the growth of some of the other churches where he had presented seminars. Glen Coleman was the preacher at the Rockview church, and the church was averaging just over 700 in weekly attendance. Bob thankfully and eagerly accepted the invitation.

The Saturday morning when he was to leave for the seminar Bob said "Kathy, I'm going to go down to Taylor's garage and have the car serviced." She responded "Why in the world are you doing that today, we've got to be in Rockview this evening?" "I know," Bob answered, "But my first session isn't until five o'clock this evening. Elvin Taylor has serviced the car for years, and he tells me if I bring it in on Saturday morning he can save me money. They open on

Saturday's only for friends and can save them money, because he and his brother have agreed that any work they do on a Saturday will not be at the regular rate. Each one of them charges whatever they want rather than the rate agreed on by the partnership. This gives them the opportunity to help those they want to give a bit of a break. Elvin has invited me to come in and get an oil change, a tune up if we need it, get the car checked out and have us set for a while." Kathy said "I still don't know why you have to do that today." Bob told her "Elvin has joined the Navy. He'll be leaving Monday to report for duty. This is the last chance we will have to take advantage of his offer."

Bob took the car, got it serviced, and came back in time for lunch before he and Kathy left for Rockview. It was a pleasant two hour drive. Kathy was in one of her best moods in months. They told jokes, sang hymns and enjoyed the scenery. They arrived in plenty of time for Bob's five o'clock session. He was to lead one session at five, the group would then have dinner, and Bob would lead a second session at seven. In his two teaching sessions he stressed that nothing was more important for church growth than a spiritual and committed leadership. He maintained that elders should be fully committed men, to be shepherds, the pastors of the flock with a deep compassion for the people, to fit the qualification for elders described in Scripture, to be continually growing in their own spiritual lives, and to be willing to sacrifice for the flock they served. "After all," he said, "Our example, the Great Shepherd, laid down His life for His sheep." He contended that they should not be encumbered with incidental matters that so often consume the time and energy of elders, but be wise enough to delegate these to deacons. The deacons, he maintained, were not selected just because there was a slot on the ballot that needed to be filled, but because there was an active ministry to be fulfilled. He pointed out that the same word that is translated "deacon" in the

THE STORM BREAKS

Bible is used over eighty times in reference to a ministry or service. He did not oppose a stated time for electing deacons, but contended that they were not be elected only because the calendar called for it, but because there was a needed function to be filled.

Bob was aware that the congregation, with the exception of Kathy, was following him closely. When Bob glanced at her, he noticed she was nodding off.

The people's response thrilled Bob. They listened intently, and at the closing time for comments and questions the participation was so positive and spirited that they had to call the first session to a close to go to dinner. The questions and comments after the second session, which began at seven o'clock, went on until nearly nine o'clock. Bob felt the Lord had used him effectively, but his satisfaction was quickly deflated when he talked with his wife. Her attitude had done a complete reversal from the pleasant demeanor she had shown on their trip to Rockview.

Kathy, whom he noticed had slept through much of his lecture, said, "I sure didn't find that very inspiring tonight. My dad would have done a much better job. And why do you have to show off so much?"

"What do you mean show off" Bob asked?

"Well, for one thing I don't know why you don't relax and be more comfortable? Why do you have to wear that strangle rag, anyway?" Kathy said.

"Strangle rag, What in the world do you mean strangle rag?" Bob asked.

Your necktie," said Kathy. "Most of the men just had open-collared shirts. I don't know why you have to be so stiff and stuffy."

Bob said, "Yes, I know most of the men did have open-collared shirts, but some of them, I would say about a third of the men, did have neckties. When I don't know what the dress expectations of the congregation are, I feel more comfortable if I'm a little overdressed than if I'm too casual."

"Well," responded Kathy, "Do as you like, but I still believe you need to loosen up."

That night Bob and Kathy were entertained by Clyde and Elizabeth Norton. They were gracious hosts, and although Kathy sat silent most of the evening, Bob had a warm fellowship and conversation with the Nortons. Before bed, they were served a dish of ice cream, and Bob and Kathy retired. Bob spent some time trying to fall asleep. He had been gratified with the way his teaching sessions had gone, but was puzzled why Kathy's attitude had changed so much from their delightful trip to Rockview to her critical attitude after the sessions. He lay in the bed mentally going over what he would preach in the morning, and then quoting several of the passages of Scripture that he found so helpful when his troubled mind had difficulty shutting down.

In the morning they were served a delightful breakfast by the Norton's and the conversation with them was stimulating. Because of Kathy's words the night before Bob debated about wearing a coat and tie for the morning worship, but on his preference to be a bit over dressed rather than too casual, he decided he would wear his suit. He was glad he did, as most of the men came in suits or sport coats and ties.

Though it was September, Indian Summer had come, and it was a hot, sunny day. When they parked at the church building Bob said, "It doesn't look like rain, so let's roll down the windows and put the sun shield against the windshield." They did this, and walked into the building. For the message, Bob preached from I John 5:4, "This is the victory that has overcome the world–our faith."

THE STORM BREAKS

In contrast to the strong sense of communication he had felt during his lectures the day before, he did not feel he was connecting with his audience. Having preached as long as he had, Bob knew that there were times when the "vibes" were positive when you preached, and other times when that dynamic just seemed to be missing. This seemed to be like the latter. He couldn't understand why, because he had chosen his topic with an excitement about preaching it, and had prepared well.

Through the meal that he and the congregation enjoyed together after the service, Bob tried to comfort himself by remembering that there had been many times before when he felt that his message had not gotten through but folks would later tell him how much that message or something he had said in it had helped them in their spiritual journey. He prayed that this might be true in this case. Still, as they were leaving the building, he was disappointed with himself. Kathy didn't help matters when she said, "Well, I'm glad that's over. You sure weren't at your best today. I just want to get home."

As they were leaving the church building, the treasurer of the church handed Bob an envelope. Bob handed it to Kathy. When they got to the car, Bob opened the door for Kathy, took off his coat and tie, and as he was walking to the driver's side of the car, Kathy nearly exploded. "This is almost an insult. Bob, I don't know why you keep doing these things."

"What do you mean?" Bob asked. Kathy answered, "This is the check for your services. One hundred and fifty dollars. You prepared and delivered two lectures and one sermon, you make a two hundred mile round trip, and this is all they pay you. I think this is outrageous."

Bob had many times bit his lip and refrained from speaking when Kathy had such outbursts, but this time he could not contain himself. As he slid into the driver's seat and he and Kathy were folding up the sun shield they had put before the windshield he answered harshly. "Kathy, you've GOT to overcome your negativism. That check will more than cover our expenses. We had what I consider a rich fellowship with these people, they were gracious hosts, we made some new friends, I had an opportunity to serve, and besides, my regular salary was paid by the church back home, even though they had to pay a supply preacher today. I am not going to put up with your negativism and criticism any more."

As Bob was putting the key into the ignition, he noticed that Elizabeth Norton had come to their still open window. Bob felt a flush of shame for his outburst. Mrs. Norton said, "I just wanted to say goodbye to you before you started home, and to tell you what a joy it was last evening to have both of you in our home. We do hope we'll be seeing you again in the future."

Bob expressed his thanks to Mrs. Norton, and as she walked away he turned to Kathy and said, "Honey, I'm sorry for my irritation. I know you are having a difficult time, and I try to be patient, but I have to admit sometimes the stress is almost more than I can bear." Kathy did not respond, and they drove off in silence.

Bob opened his eyes and realized he was looking straight up. As he struggled to wake up, he recognized the ceiling with the channels that suspended the curtains which were used to separate the beds to be the ceiling of a patient room in the Medical Center.

A voice said, "Good morning, Mr. Morganton." Bob looked into the face of the nurse who stood beside his bed. He recognized her, but in his half awake state could not recall her name.

Slowly becoming conscious of where he was he said, "This is the Medical Center isn't it?"

"Yes," the nurse answered. "You've been here since Sunday evening."

THE STORM BREAKS

"What happened, and what time is it now?" asked Bob.

"You were in an accident, and it is now 6:45 on Tuesday morning" answered nurse Beth Harper.

"Tuesday morning, and I've been here since Sunday?"

"Yes," said the nurse. "And you'll be here for a few days more. You've had a concussion, you have a broken knee, two broken ribs and a lot of other bruises. You were unconscious for several hours from the concussion, and when you came out of it enough for us to administer sedatives, we did, and we have had you under sedation because of the pain."

"Where is Kathy, and how is she?" Bob asked.

Nurse Harper was obviously shaken. When she was able to speak she said, "I'm sorry, Mr. Morganton. Kathy didn't survive the accident."

Bob turned his face away from the voice, as though that would silence the news he was hearing. He closed his eyes as he felt the tears begin to flow. In his still nearly unconscious state he was trying hard to process what he had just heard. He thought, "I must be dreaming, this cannot be real." Mercifully, soon the heavy sedation put him back asleep.

Bob spent several hours in semi-consciousness. He would awaken for a while, weep, and then fall back into a fitful slumber.

The reality set in at about 9:40, when Karen came just before she began her shift at the Medical Center at 10 a.m. She took Bob's hand, and they wept together. Then Roger Jones and Clarence White, two elders of the church came to visit. They prayed with Bob for his recovery, and for the surpassing peace God promises to His children to sustain Bob at the loss of his wife. Tuesday evening John Black and Jerry Johnson, the other two elders, came with their wives to visit and pray for Bob. They told him that they had arranged for another preacher to take care of the pulpit responsibilities for as long as needed, and that Bob should not worry about things at the church, but just concentrate on healing. In the midst of his heartbreak Bob was finding strength as the family of God surrounded him with their love and concern.

Later that evening, just before visiting hours ended, Leroy Henson. the county Sheriff, came into the room. Bob and the Sheriff were personal friends, on a first name basis with each other.

"Bob," said Sheriff Henson, "I know you've been through a real rough couple of days, and I hated to come now, but the doctors and nurses said they thought it would be all right to talk with you now. I can't tell you how grieved my wife and I are at Kathy's death, and the suffering, both physical and mental, that you're going through. We are following up and making our report on your accident, and we need to know what happened."

Bob said, "I won't be of much help. I don't know what happened, I can't recall it at all."

The Sheriff said, "You ran into that huge oak just alongside the highway about three miles from here.

Your car was totaled, and has been hauled away. We can't figure out what caused the accident. We found no skid marks or evidence of what may have caused you to go off the road there? Was there another vehicle involved? Were you forced off the road? Did you fall asleep?"

"I'm sorry Leroy," said Bob. "The last thing I remember is leaving the church in Rockview at about 1:15 Sunday afternoon. The next thing I knew I was waking up here this morning."

"Well, I'm sorry to have bothered you this soon," said the Sheriff. "I'll let you get some rest now, and talk to you again later. I want you to know that I, and my deputies, are all praying for you."

THE STORM BREAKS

Thursday morning Sheriff Henson returned, and this time Bob was surprised that a state trooper was with him. The sheriff said, "Bob, we're still mystified about the cause of your accident Sunday. That's a state highway where it occurred, and the state is now involved in the investigation. All we can conclude is that you must have fallen asleep. Do you remember any more about it?"

Bob thought as hard as he could. Then he said, "Dr. Moreland told me that my memory would probably all come back in time, but that it would probably return in stages. As I try to recreate in my mind what happened, it seems that I swerved to miss something, perhaps an animal in the road. If it clears up in my mind, I'll surely let you know."

The sheriff took Bob's hand, gave him as firm a grip as he could without hurting him and said, "Thanks Bob. Remember the boys and I down at the station still pray for you everyday."

As Karen came in each day they made plans for Kathy's funeral. They decided to wait until the Thursday of the following week. That would give time for Kathy's brothers, Lester and Alvin Bailey, and their families to make plans and be there. It would also hopefully give enough time for Bob to recover sufficiently to be out of the hospital and attend the funeral. It was decided that the funeral service would be a time of celebration of Kathy's life. They were determined to remember her as she was in her happier days, when her life had been a glowing testimony of faith, joy and positive influence on everyone she met.

And it was exactly that. While there were tears of sadness, there was also laughter as some of the joyous and even humorous episodes of Kathy's life were recalled.

Lester told a story from the girls' childhood he had heard from their mother. Kathy and Karen were in their room, and Mrs. Bailey heard one of them say, "It's 42." "No," answered the other, "It's 44". One would say "It's left," and the other, "I'm sure it's right." "It's north." "No it's not, it's south." Her curiosity aroused, Mrs. Bailey entered the room and asked "What are you girls doing?" They answered, "We're playing the game Grandma and Grandpa play when they travel."

Alvin Bailey told of a time when the girls had been learning the Ten Commandments in Sunday school. Kathy had found that she could at times gain an advantage by bending the facts a bit. Her parents had talked to her about taking more care to be honest about things. One day Karen burst into the house shouting "Mom, Kathy broke the eighth commandment." Kathy was right behind her, and exclaimed "Uh uh, it was the ninth!" (9)

Bob, from a wheel chair, spoke on a more somber note. Through tears he told of the wonderful helpmeet Kathy had been to him during the first couple years of their ministry. He told of her valiant struggle after the loss of their baby and death of her father and deteriorating health to still serve in any way she could. He gave thanks that though the past couple of years of her life had been so hard she was now was in a place where sorrow and pain and tears would be no more.

Denver Newton, Bob's good friend from the Hillsborough church, brought a most comforting message from John 11:25 where Jesus said, "I am the resurrection and the life. He that believes on Me, though he die, yet shall he live."

Sheriff Henson himself drove a squad car to escort the large funeral procession to the cemetery. After the graveside service as Bob, in a wheel chair, Lester, Alvin and Karen were returning to the cars, Bob noticed that with Sheriff Henson were one of his deputies and the state trooper who had come to the hospital with him. They were not in uniform, but in plain clothes. The sheriff said, "Bob, official procedure is for me to handcuff you now, and take you to the police station, but I'll trust you and not do that. However you have to promise within the hour you'll come to the police station. My squad car will follow you to make sure you do that. Personally, I can't believe you're guilty, but I have to arrest you for the murder of your wife."

Bob was astonished. "How can that be, Leroy?" he asked.

The Sheriff answered, "There is strong evidence that your car crash was not an accident. You're charged with Vehicular Homicide in Kathy's death."

THE TRIAL

During the days while they were waiting for the trial to begin, Sheriff Henson talked with Bob several times. He told him that the state had taken over the case, and were going to send a state prosecutor. He informed Bob that the question they had not answered was what caused Bob to run off the highway in broad daylight at a time and place where there seemed to be no other traffic. Bob told him "My memory has pretty much returned. I was not asleep, although Kathy was. That animal that was so foggy in my mind before I now clearly remember was a large pig or hog. It came from the opposite side of the road, and was running at an angle into my lane. I guess my knee jerk reaction must have been to swerve off the road."

As the trial unfolded, it was clear Arthur Cline, the state prosecutor, had prepared well and done an amazing amount of research and interviewing. The first witness he called was deputy Clyde Wilman of the county sheriff's office. He asked him, "Deputy Wilman, you were the first officer to examine the accident scene, weren't you?"

"Yes, that is correct" said the deputy

"And was there anything unusual about that scene?" questioned Mr. Cline.

Deputy Wilman answered, "It seemed odd to me that there was no evidence of any other vehicle being involved, and that there were

THE TRIAL

no skid marks indicating that brakes had been applied before the car hit the tree."

Mr. Cline said, "Did it appear to you that possibly that car had been driven purposely into that tree with no effort to avoid it?"

"It occurred to me that could have been the case," said the deputy.

"And would you describe how you found the passengers in the car, Mr. Wilman?"

Deputy Wilman responded: "Mr. Morganton was in the driver's seat, unconscious but alive. Mrs. Morganton was in the front passenger seat. When the EMS team arrived they put both Mr. Morganton and Mrs. Morganton in an ambulance, but said they found no signs of life in Mrs. Morganton."

Mr. Cline said, "Would you tell us how the seat belts and air bags were when you arrived?"

Deputy Wilman answered, "Mr. Morganton's seat belt was fastened, and his air bag had deployed. Mrs. Morganton's seat belt was unbuckled, and her air bag had not deployed."

"I have no further questions," said prosecutor Cline.

The state had offered to pay for an attorney to represent Mr. Morganton. However, Ronald Reese, an attorney who was in the congregation at Hillsborough where Bob's good friend Denver Newton preached had offered to defend Bob for a fraction of his usual fee. Even though Bob realized this would still be a financial challenge to him, he employed Ronald Reese, and declined the state's offer.

Ronald Reese said, "Your Honor, I have no questions at this time, but retain the privilege to call this witness at another time."

Arthur Cline next called nurse Beth Harper to the stand and asked her, "You were the nurse present when Mr. Morganton first regained consciousness after his accident, were you not?"

"That's true," responded the nurse.

"And what was Mr. Morganton's first reaction when you told him his wife had died? Did he seemed surprised?"

"No, not that I could tell," said Miss Harper.

Mr. Cline continued, "Could you tell us then how he reacted?"

Beth Harper said, "He turned his head away from me, and in a few moments fell asleep."

"No further questions," said the prosecutor.

In defense Mr. Reese asked, "Miss Harper, is it not possible that Mr. Morganton's apparently unmoved reaction to the news of his wife's death could be attributed to a number of factors, things like the fact that he was still heavily sedated, or that he was in shock at the news, or that in such a state he could not immediately comprehend or accept or process such information? Could not his physical and mental state at such a time explain what you felt was an indifferent reaction?"

"Yes, I suppose any one of those could explain it," Beth answered.

"No further questions, your Honor," said Mr. Reese.

Mr. Cline then called Mrs. Elizabeth Norton to the witness stand. As she passed where Bob was seated she gently laid a hand on his shoulder.

After she had taken her oath and was seated, Mr. Cline said, "Mrs. Norton, I want to remind you that you are under oath, and that failure to honestly answer any questions I ask will be considered contempt of court or perjury. "Mrs. Norton," he asked, "what is your relationship to Mr. Morganton?"

Elizabeth answered," It has been limited. They were in our home overnight a few weeks ago."

Mr. Cline then asked, "I understand that you were the last person to speak with them as they were leaving to return home that Sunday afternoon."

"That is correct," Elizabeth answered.

Mr. Cline said, "Could you tell the court about that conversation?"

Elizabeth replied, "I stepped to their car to tell them what a pleasure it had been to meet them and to have them in our home."

"And did you hear any of the conversation between Mr. and Mrs. Morganton?" was Mr. Cline's next question.

Elizabeth Norton looked downward and hesitated. It was obvious she did not want to answer.

Mr. Cline said, "I remind you, Mrs. Norton that you have been issued a summons to appear in this court, and by law are obligated to answer all questions honestly. What did you hear of their conversation?" Very haltingly Elizabeth replied, "I heard Mr. Morganton say, 'I am not going to put up with this criticism any longer."

Mr. Cline then asked, "And what did you feel Mr. Morganton's attitude was when he made that remark?"

"Objection!" cried Ronald Reese, "calls for speculation."

"Sustained," said Judge Harold Downs.

Mr. Cline continued, "Let me rephrase. Was Mr. Morganton irritated when he made that remark?"

"Objection! Still calls for speculation.," said Mr. Reese.

Again Judge Downs said, "Sustained."

"Let me try once more." said Mr. Cline. "Would you say Mr. Morganton's tone of voice was mellow or harsh as he spoke?"

Elizabeth said, "I suppose harsh, however...."

"No further questions, your, Honor." said Mr. Cline.

When Mr. Reese arose to cross examine he asked, "Mrs. Norton, are you sure those were Mr. Morganton's exact words?"

Mrs. Norton answered, "I'm not sure of the exact words, but I know that's essentially what he said. It may have been 'I won't listen to your negativism any longer', or something like that."

"I have no further questions your Honor but again I reserve permission to call this witness later."

Next the prosecuting attorney called Mr. Samuel Belton.

"Mr. Belton, I understand you are the owner of Sam's Auto Salvage, is that correct?" said Mr. Cline.

"Yes Sir," answered Mr. Belton.

"And I believe you towed the Morganton car to your salvage lot, and still have it there." said Mr. Cline.

"That's correct."

"And would you describe the damage on that car?"

Mr. Belton answered, "It was totally wrecked."

Mr. Cline continued his questioning "Did the car strike that tree right in the middle of the front bumper?"

"No, it impacted right of center, just inside the right headlight." said Sam.

"On the passenger side then?" questioned Mr. Cline.

"Yes." was Sam's reply.

"Would this be likely then, in your opinion, to be more apt to cause more injury to a person in the passenger seat than to one in the driver's seat?" was Mr. Cline's next question.

"Objection, calls for opinion," said Mr. Reese.

Again Judge Downs said, "Sustained."

Mr. Cline tried one more time. "Mr. Belton, in your experience have you observed that impacts on the front of the passenger side of the car cause more injuries to those on the passenger side than on the driver's side?" Mr. Belton responded, "I can't recall any personal observation about that because we get the cars long after the

THE TRIAL

passengers have been removed from them, but it would seem logical that would be the case–that those on the side of the impact would be more likely to suffer greater injury, or even death."

"Thank you Mr. Belton." No further questions.

Mr. Reese began his cross examination. "Mr. Belton, I understand that what you have said about greater damage to the passenger side is based on no particular experience or observation, but only what you think would seem logical. Is that right?"

Mr. Belton answered, "That's right, I have no personal observation or information to verify my opinion."

Mr. Reese said, "Thank you Mr. Belton, I have no further questions. However, I would remind the court that the point of impact in this accident was at the front, and not on the side of the car."

Judge Downs adjourned the court for the day, but said the trial would reconvene at 9 A.M. the next day.

Orville Nelson was the editor of the <u>Conner's Crossing Crier</u>, a small paper that came out twice weekly. In the weeks to follow he would report in almost every issue news of the trial, and his comments were sympathetic toward Bob. However, the trial had now gained wide attention, and other newpapers in the state were almost merciless in their obvious anticipation of a guilty verdict. One paper even titled it, "The Case of the Murdering Minister."

When the trial resumed, prosecutor Arthur Cline first called Ellen Bridgewell to the witness stand.

He asked, "Ms. Bridgewell, are you a member of the church where Robert Morganton preaches?"

She answered, "Yes Sir, I have been for years."

Mr. Cline continued, "Would you describe yourself as an active member?"

Ms. Bridgewell responded. "Yes, I lead the women's ministry, and I attend every scheduled service of the church I possibly can."

Mr. Cline asked, "Can we understand then that you have the best interest of the church at heart?"

Ms. Bridgewell said, "Absolutely."

Mr. Cline then said, "Ms. Bridgewell, have you ever seen anything that deeply concerned you about your preacher, Mr. Morganton?"

"Yes," she responded. One morning in May, I don't recall the exact date, I was entering the church building just as Kathy Morganton came marching out, evidently in quite a huff. I asked her what was wrong, and she said, "That husband of mine is the most stubborn and unreasonable man I've ever met."

"Is there any other thing that disturbed you?" asked the prosecutor.

"There certainly is," answered Ms. Bridgewell. On Tuesday, June 11th, as I was entering the church building to prepare for our women's bi-weekly Bible study I stopped by Mr. Morganton's study to ask him if we were to meet in our usual room. As I stepped into the doorway I saw Mr. Morganton and Karen Bailey, his sister-in-law, in an embrace and kissing."

Ronald Reese, Bob's attorney, looked shocked and whispered to Bob, "What's this all about? You didn't tell me about this."

Bob said, "There's a simple explanation. We can clear that up in cross examination." Arthur Cline continued with his questioning: Ms. Bridgewell, will you also tell us what you saw in Mr. Morganton's home on the morning of July 5th?"

"Yes," was her reply. "Early on the morning of July 5th I went to the Morganton's to pick up Kathy and Karen for our annual shopping spree at Bellville. Several stores over there have a big sale the day after Independence Day. They send out mailers with coupons that have considerable savings, and Kathy, Karen and I have kind of made this

THE TRIAL

an annual tradition. I had called Kathy the evening of July 4th to ask if she felt up to the trip, and she said she thought she did. We leave early to try to get there before the best bargains are all gone. When I arrived at about 6:30 Kathy was in the kitchen making coffee. There was a pillow and a blanket on the couch, and I asssumed that Kathy had slept there, as she frequently does. She said she would be ready in a few minutes, and that Karen had the sales coupons, and asked me to go up to her room to see if Karen was ready to leave, and to make sure we had the coupons. As I approached the stairway Bob and Kathy's bedroom door was open, and it was evident that no one had slept in the bed. The bedspread was in place, but it was rumpled as though someone had laid on top the bed, but it was evident no one had gotten under the covers. The bedspread was still over the pillows. Then I saw Mr. Morganton coming out of Karen's bedroom, and down the stairs."

Mr. Cline asked, "What was he wearing?"

"A bathrobe," Ms. Bridgewell answered.

"And what else?" asked Mr. Cline.

"I could not tell, the bathrobe was all I saw."

"Did Mr. Morganton say anything to you?" asked the prosecutor.

"Yes," answered Ms. Bridgewell. "He looked very sheepish, and said 'Karen is not well today. She won't be going with you to Bellville."

Mr. Cline's next question was, "Did he make any explanation as to why he had been in Karen's bedroom?"

"No, he just passed me and went into his bedroom."

"What was your impression of all this?" said Mr. Cline.

"Objection!" cried Mr. Reese, "Calls for speculation."

"Sustained," said Judge Downs.

Mr. Cline went on: "Ms. Bridgewell, in your years of friendship with Kathy Morganton have you ridden in a car with her?"

"Yes, many times," Ms. Bridgewell answered.

Mr. Cline: "And would you tell us was it Kathy's practice to always fasten her seat belt?"

Ms. Bridgewell: "Very much so. She was insistent on this, and if she were driving she would not start the engine until everyone in the car was buckled in. She was nearly fanatical about this. In fact we dubbed her 'the enforcer' because she was so adamant about seat belts."

Mr. Cline asked: "Would she then have been riding that Sunday afternoon with her seat belt unbuckled?"

"No way," responded Ms. Bridgewell.

"I have no further questions." said Arthur Cline.

Ronald Reese said "Your Honor, I would like a few minutes to confer with my client before I cross examine."

"Granted" said Judge Downs. "The court will recess for twenty minutes." When the court reconvened, Ronald Reese called Ms. Bridgewell to the witness stand again. He asked, "Ms. Bridgewell, you said you saw Mr. Morganton and Karen Bailey kissing and embracing. How long were they in that embrace?"

Ms. Bridgewell answered, "Well, as soon as they saw me, they separated."

Mr. Reese proceeded: "And you said you saw them kissing? Were they lip to lip?"

Ms. Bridgewell replied, "Well, I couldn't see for sure, but I know their faces were touching."

Mr. Reese said, "Ms. Bridgewell, Mr. Morganton tells me that Karen Bailey had just stepped off a step-stool and had turned an ankle. As she lunged forward, he caught her to keep her from falling. Could that innocent act explain what you thought was a kiss and embrace?"

Ms. Bridgewell's response was, "Well, that's what they told me at the time, but I found it hard to believe. Their embrace seemed to me to be more intentional than that."

Mr. Reese's next question was, "Ms. Bridgewell, did you see a step-stool near where they were?"

Ms. Bridgewell replied, "I don't recall seeing one."

Mr. Reese asked, "could you say with confidence that there was no step-stool there?"

"No, I couldn't say that for certain, but I don't recall seeing it there," Ms. Bridgewell responded.

Mr. Reese's next question was, "You mentioned seeing Mr. Morganton coming from Karen Bailey's room on the morning of July 5th. Did you see him open the door to come out?"

"No," replied Ms. Bridgewell. "When I first saw him he was already in the doorway."

"It is possible then," continued Mr. Reese, "that while he was in the room the door had been open?"

"Well, I suppose so." was Ms. Bridgewell's answer.

"Your Honor," said Mr. Reese, "I'm am going to call Mr. Morganton later to tell us precisely why he had been in Karen's bedroom, but I have a few more questions for Ms. Bridgewell just now." Turning again to

Ms. Bridgewell he asked, "Did you go into Karen's bedroom after you passed Mr. Morganton?"

"Yes," she answered.

"And what did you see there?" queried Mr. Reese.

"Karen was still asleep," she said. "I saw the coupons on Karen's dressing table, picked them up, and went to Karen's bedside. She stirred, and I asked her if she was going with us to Bellville. She said she was tired, didn't feel well, and thought she had better stay home."

"Tell us what happened next?" said Mr. Reese.

Ms. Bridgewell answered, "I went down and told Kathy that Karen was not going, and we decided we would not go either. Bob came into the kitchen a little later, we ate breakfast, and Bob left for his study at the church building."

Mr. Reese asked, "Did you tell Kathy about Bob being in Karen's bedroom?"

"No," replied Ms. Bridgewell

"Why not?" asked Mr. Reese.

Ms. Bridgewell answered, "When I saw the earlier episode with Bob and Karen in his study, and even though others were told of it, it never seemed to phase Kathy. I don't know if no one told her in order to spare her from hurt or if she heard it and ignored it. At any rate, I chose not to tell Kathy at this time."

Mr. Reese continued his questions. "Ms. Bridgewell, think hard. When you were in Karen's room did you notice the chair at Karen's dressing table? Was it positioned facing the dressing table, or was it turned away from it?"

Ms. Bridgewell paused thoughtfully for quite a while. Then she answered "I believe it was turned away from the mirror and was facing the bed."

"Did this not seem a bit strange to you?" Mr. Reese asked Ms. Bridgewell.

Again Ms. Bridgewell hesitated, then responded, "No, it seemed the likely position if someone were leaving the dressing table to go to bed."

"I have no futher questions at this time, but retain the right to call her again later," said Mr. Reese.

Arthur Cline, the prosecutor, then called sheriff Leroy Henson to the witness stand. After taking the oath he was asked, "Sheriff

Henson, I understand you were the first law officer to talk with Mr. Morganton after the accident. Is this correct?"

"Yes, that is correct." answered the sheriff.

"When you first asked Mr. Morganton what had caused him to leave the road and hit that tree how did he answer?" was the next question.

"At that time he told me he had no recollection, and that his doctor had said it may be some time until his memory cleared up" said the sheriff.

"And did you ask him again later?" asked Mr. Cline.

"Yes Sir, I did. In fact, a couple of times," he responded.

"And what were his answers then?" asked Mr. Cline.

In response Sheriff Henson answered, "A couple of days later Bob, excuse me, Mr. Morganton, told me that he had a foggy recollection of some animal coming into the road and he swerved to miss it. Then later as his memory had cleared he told me he clearly remembered that it had been a large pig or hog."

"Sheriff Henson," said Mr. Cline with a clear tone of skepticism, "did he make the identification of a hog or pig before or after his arrest?"

"It was after he was arrested, and before this trial began, but Mr. Cline I have a strong confidence in Bob's integrity, and.....," began the sheriff's reply.

The prosecutor cut him off with his next question. "And has there been any attempt to verify the likelihood of that being the case in that area? Has there been any attempt to find pig farms near where the accident took place?"

"Yes, there has been, Sir. The police have questioned every farmer within two miles of the spot."

The prosecutor pressed on. "And how many pig farms are there in a radius of two miles?"

"None, however....."

Again the prosecutor cut off the witness. "Sheriff Henson, I'm sure you are aware of recent studies that show how strong an impact with a solid object, like that oak tree this car hit, can be survived by passengers in a car with air bags if their seat belts are fastened. Would you tell the court what those studies reveal?"

"Yes," said the sheriff. "With air bags and seat belts the survival rate is high in an impact up to 50 miles per hour."

"And," continued Mr. Cline, "what is the survival rate in such a collision if the car does not have air bags and seat belts are not fastened?"

Sheriff Henson answered, "In such a case the survival rate is low; the fatality rate is very high."

"Sheriff," Mr. Cline asked, "as you and your deputies examined the scene of the accident and the condition of the car, how fast did you estimate Mr. Morganton was driving when they struck that tree?"

The sheriff seemed hesitant to answer. "Forty-five to fifty miles per hour" he said.

"Thank you, I have no further questions" said prosecutor Cline.

In his cross examination Ronald Reese tried hard to find some way to soften the impact of the sheriff's testimony, but it was clear Mr. Cline and the evidence he had compiled had been powerfully convincing.

The court recessed for the day. As the defense began it's case the next morning, Mr. Reese first called Karen Bailey to the stand.

"Miss Bailey," he began, "would you tell us in your own words what happened the night of July 4th and the morning of July 5th?"

"I will," Karen said, "although much of it is unclear to me. Bob and Kathy and I came home from the Fourth of July celebration in the park quite early. We didn't even stay for the fireworks because I was feeling odd and Kathy was quite tired. I went to bed early, and don't remember much of the night, although I woke up aware that someone else had been in the room most of the night. They told me I had blacked out the night before, and that they had called Dr. Moreland, and he told them what to do. I woke up quite disoriented. Ellen Bridgewell came to my bedside and asked if I still wanted to go on our shopping trip to Bellville, and I said I thought maybe I'd better stay home. I felt very weak and slept all day. In fact it wasn't until evening of the following day that I felt much better."

In his cross examination Mr. Cline said, "You told us you were aware that someone had been in the room with you through the night. Karen, was the 'someone' in bed with you anytime during that night? And could that someone have been Robert Morganton?"

Karen flushed with anger. "No, I would have known if anyone had been in bed with me, and I don't know who the person in the room was. I deeply resent your insinuation, Sir."

Judge Downs said, "Be careful, Mr. Cline. And Miss Bailey, just answer the questions."

Prosecutor Cline continued: "Miss Bailey, will you tell me of your relationship with Mr. Morganton?"

"Certainly," Karen responded. "He is my brother-in-law, and preaches at our church."

Mr. Cline: "And what is your personal feeling about him?"

Karen: "I respect and admire him."

Mr. Cline: "Does your feeling for him ever go beyond just admiration and respect? Do you have any feelings of a more than usual attraction for him?"

Karen: "Well, I cannot honestly say that I do not find him attractive, but if you're asking if our relationship has ever gone beyond being in-laws and good friends, the answer is no."

Mr. Cline: "I understand that for a time Kathy, Mrs. Morganton, assisted Mr. Morganton in his office work, and that you replaced her and worked with Mr. Morganton at the church office. Is that correct?"

Karen: "Yes, for a short time."

Mr. Cline: "And was Mrs. Morganton paid for her asistance to her husband?"

Karen: "Yes Sir, she received a very small stipend for her work."

Mr. Cline: "And were you paid for your assistance to him?"

Karen: "No, after Kathy felt she could not work there anymore, I volunteered to help out for just a very few hours a week without pay."

Mr. Cline: "I see. Mrs. Morganton was paid for her work, but you admired and respected Mr. Morganton so much that you were willing to work close to him for no pay. Very interesting."

Judge Downs said, "That will be enough, Mr. Cline. Please confine your statements to questions."

The prosecutor then asked: "Miss Bailey did you continue to work long as a volunteer for Mr. Morganton?"

"No, only a few weeks," Karen answered.

"And can you tell me why you stopped your volunteer work?" asked Mr. Cline.

Karen replied, "Because we became aware that with Kathy no longer coming into the office there may have been some who questioned the propriety of my being there. We yielded to their concerns."

Mr. Cline asked, "And were those concerns justified?"

"Abolutely not!" Karen shot back angrily.

"No more questions," said Mr. Cline.

After Mr. Cline's questioning of Karen Bailey, Ronald Reese had another opportunity to question her. He began by asking, "Miss Bailey, you have also often ridden with your sister Kathy in an automobile, haven't you?"

"Yes, many times." Karen answered.

Mr. Reese continued, "You have heard the testimony of Ms. Bridgewell that Kathy was a fanatic about seat belts, and was always insistent that they be buckled. Have you any observation about that testimony?"

Karen responded: "During most of her life that was very true. However, everyone who knew Kathy also knows that during the last years of her life many things about her changed. She became complacent about many things that she had previously been very adamant about. She was riding with me one day and I noticed she hadn't buckled her belt, and I said, 'Sis, aren't you going to buckle in?' Her response was, 'Well, if God can't take care of me, what good is a silly seat belt going to do?'

"No more questions," said Mr. Reese.

Ronald Reese then called Robert Morganton to the stand. After taking the oath, Bob was asked, "You heard Miss Bailey's explanation of what took place on the night of July 4th. Could you tell us in your own words what happened?"

"Gladly," said Bob. "Karen, Kathy and I had gone to the city park for the Fourth of July celebration. We visited the booths, some of the refreshment stands, listened to some of the musical groups, and spent a good deal of time just talking with friends, most of them in our church family. We had planned to stay for the fireworks display, but as dusk came on Kathy said she was very tired, and Karen said she wasn't feeling very well either, said she felt a little dizzy, so we went home and sat on our porch where we watched more of the fireworks–those that were highest in the sky we could see quite well. When the fireworks ended, Kathy went in on the couch, as she often does, Karen went to her room to go to bed. I sat on the porch for a little while, and when I went in Kathy was sound asleep on the couch. It was still a warm night, she had no blankets over her, but I folded a sheet and put it where she could pull it up easily if she wanted to before morning. I went to our bedroom, turned on the TV, laid down on top of the bed and watched the 10 o'clock news. Just as I was turning off the TV, I heard a thud from Karen's upstairs bedroom. I hurried up there and found Karen unconscious on the floor. I picked her up, and put her back in her bed. Then I called Dr. Moreland from Karen's bedroom phone."

"I told the doctor what had happened, and asked if I should take her to the Medical Center. He said, 'First let me ask you some questions.' Then he asked, 'Were you in the city park for the festivities on the 3rd and 4th?' I told him we had been there on the 4th, and he said, 'Take Karen's temperature and her pulse.' I did, and told him her temperature was 101, and her pulse 65. He then asked me if her breathing was regular, and I told him it was. He said 'I'm almost certain what this is. A strange kind of thing has broken out among many of the community who were at the park the past couple of days. I wouldn't advise you to go to the Medical Center because when I left there this evening their beds were all filled because of this strange bug. However, thank the Lord, this thing is not serious. It only lasts about 24 to 36 hours. Those who came in early on the 3rd are getting better already and are about to be released by morning. I would advise you to keep Karen where she is, try to get plenty of liquids in her, and keep checking her temperature and pulse, and observe her breathing. That's about all they're doing with those who came to the Center. If her temperature goes up, or if there is a noticable change in her pulse rate or if her breathing becomes labored or irregular, call me back."

"I thanked Dr. Moreland, and went down and told Kathy what had happened, and asked her to come up to Karen's room, and we would watch her through the night. Kathy answered, barely coherent, that she would, got off the couch and staggered to the bathroom, still very sleepy, or perhaps sedated.

I filled a glass of water and went back upstairs to Karen's room. I managed to get her to take a little water, and since Kathy had not come up yet, I went back downstairs. Kathy was back on the couch, sound asleep again. I went back to Karen's room, turned her dressing table chair toward the bed, and sat down. I dozed some through the night, waking often and checking on Karen. Her temperature, pulse and breathing remained constant. In the morning I heard Ms. Bridgewell come in and talk with Kathy. As I was coming out of Karen's room and starting down the stairs, I passed Ms. Bridgewell."

Mr. Cline began his cross examination.

Mr. Cline said: "You are Reverend Robert Morganton, isn't that right?"

Bob: "I am Robert Morganton, but I do not use the title "Reverend," and prefer just to be called Mr. Morganton."

Mr. Cline: "And why do you not use the term "Reverend?""

Bob: "In some translations of the Bible Psalm 111:9 uses that term in reference to God, and we believe that therefore it should not be used in reference to a man. As a matter of fact, based on what Jesus said in Matt. 23:7-13 we refrain from taking any titles that would infer an ecclesiastical hierarchy."

Mr. Cline: "You say 'we believe' and 'we refrain' Are there others who feel this way, or is this a quirky idea you have?"

Bob: "There are hundreds of thousands in the fellowship which I serve, and yes, they feel this way and use the terminology I use."

Mr. Cline: "Oh, I see. And how do the members of your congregation address you then?"

Bob: "As mister, or brother, or preacher Bob."

Mr. Cline: "Well, then M I S T E R Morganton," Mr. Cline continued, his voice saturated with sarcasm, "that sounds a little backwoodsish to me. You do claim to be an ordained man of the cloth, do you not?"

Judge Downs interjected, "Mr. Cline, in this courtroom please watch your tone. We will not tolerate rudeness nor insult." Then he said to Bob, "Mr. Morganton, you may answer the question."

Bob: "Yes, I have been ordained to the Christian ministry."

Mr. Cline: "And by which denomination were you ordained?"

Bob: "None."

Mr. Cline: "Well then, what Presbytery or Synod or Diocese or Council ordained you?"

Bob: "None, in the sense in which you are using the words, although presbyters, which we understand in the Bible to be elders in a local congregation, were involved. I was ordained by the elders of my home church, the Millerville congregation. Some of the faculty from my Alma Mater, Clovernook Seminary, participated in the ordination ceremony."

Mr. Cline: "So then, you are not licensed by any national denomination or organization? I understand, however, that you have been actively involved in several community affairs in the cause of religious enterprises. Is it not true that you and your people were actively involved in opposing the opening of a casino in our county?"

THE TRIAL

Bob: "Yes Sir, that is correct."

Mr. Cline: "I would guess then, that means you oppose gambling?"

Bob: "That is true."

Mr. Cline: "How then is it that you justify personal gambling?"

Bob: "I don't."

Mr. Cline: "Mr. Morganton, I have witnesses, and some of them are even in this courtroom, whom I could call who would testify that they have observed you gambling at the Country Club. They tell me that you and three other men regularly play golf on Thursday, and that you bet on your scores."

Bob: "Well, it's true that we play, and for fun we pay a penny a hole for the holes we lose. I wouldn't exactly call that high stakes gambling."

Mr. Cline: "I have a witness who will testify that he heard one of your number say as you were totalling up your scores, 'I guess I'll have to go the bank and get a loan to pay this off.' Do you deny this?"

Bob: "I recall the incident. Jerry Johnson said that when he lost, I believe, 28 cents. (There was a ripple of laughter through the courtroom). Those in this courtroom who know Jerry Johnson and his sense of humor will understand that remark. I believe if you were to ask your witness he would acknowledge that at that remark there was laughter at the table where we were seated. We all knew it was a joke."

Mr. Cline, with a condescending tone: "Mr. Morganton, is it true that the morning before you left for your speaking engagement at the Rockview church you had your car serviced?"

Bob: "Yes, Elvin Taylor serviced it for me."

Mr. Cline: "What did you have done?"

Bob: "It was just a check up and minor tune up. He changed the oil, rotated the tires, he replaced spark plugs. I believe that was about it."

Mr. Cline: "Did he check the operation of the air bags at that time?"

Bob: "Not to my knowledge."

Mr. Cline: "Mr. Morganton, I remind you that you are under oath. Did Mr. Taylor disengage or in any way do anything to cause the right front airbag of your car to not function?"

Bob: "Not at all."

Mr. Cline: "And would Elvin Taylor testify to that fact?"

Bob: "I'm sure he would if he were here, but he is now away serving in the Navy."

Mr. Cline: "That's fortunate for you, isn't it, Mr. Morganton?"

Mr. Reese immediatly said, "Objection! He's badgering the witness."

Judge Downs said "Sustained! Please Mr. Cline, I've warned you about your attitude and tone. You will show more respect for this court."

Mr. Cline: "I apologize, your Honor." Then he turned again to Mr. Morganton: "I understand that there has been some decline in the attendance of your church lately. Is that correct?"

Bob: "I don't consider it 'my church'. I simply serve the Lord in His church. However it is true that there has been a decrease in attendance."

Mr. Cline: "And is there anything you know of that has caused that decline?"

Bob: "Yes, for one thing a large church able to provide almost any service any family could want has come to town and some of our members have gone over there."

THE TRIAL

Mr. Cline: "But is it not true that some have left because of things they have heard about you?"

Bob: "Unfortunately, that is true. There have been some rumors circulated that were based on a completely innocent situation that was blown all out of proportion. I have already spoken of that situation."

Mr. Cline: "You and Miss Bailey have already told us about the time she worked in the church office with you. I ask you, Mr. Morganton, do you find Karen Bailey attractive?"

Mr. Reese said, "Objection, your Honor, irrelevant."

Mr. Cline: "I will establish its relevancy, your Honor. It goes to motive."

Judge Downs: "I will allow the question, but I caution you again, Mr. Cline; watch yourself. Mr. Morganton, you will answer the question."

Bob: "Do I consider Karen Bailey attractive? I'm not blind, I can't think there is anyone in this courtroom who would not say she is attractive." Stifled laughs were heard through the courtroom again.

Mr. Cline: "Mr. Morganton, how attracted are you to her? Are you not in fact in love with her?"

Bob: "I remind you of my previous testimony. As a sister-in-law, and as a member of the church family I love Karen, as I do the other members of the congregation. But if you are asking if we are lovers, the answer is absolutely not."

Mr. Cline: "Is it not true that not only do you live in the same house as Miss Bailey, but you have several meals a week with her away from the house?"

Bob: "Yes, for these last several months Kathy had not wanted to cook, and I am often in the Medical Center around noon making calls, and Karen, who works at the Medical Center, and I have met

THE TRIAL

for lunch in the cafeteria there." Mr. Cline: "How sweet. I want to return to your testimony about the night you spent in Miss Bailey's bedroom. You claim you found her on the floor, put her in bed, and phoned Dr. Moreland from her bedroom. Did you call Dr. Moreland at the Medical Center or at his home?"

Bob: "At his home."

Mr. Cline: "Isn't that a bit unusual?" You said it was after the late news, so it must have been very late, perhaps approaching midnight. Isn't that awfully late to phone a doctor at his home?"

Bob: "It would have been between 10:30 and 11:00 PM, probably about 10:45. I have been close friends with Dr. Moreland for years, Karen often works with him at the Medical Center. He has told us often to call him any hour of the night or day if we have a medical emergency."

Mr. Cline: "And would Dr. Moreland concur with this, and with all you have told us about that night of July 4th until the morning of July 5th?"

Bob: "I'm sure he would if he were here, but Dr. Moreland is presently in Haiti. He goes there for about a month every year to do volunteer medical work with a missionary."

Mr. Cline, again with disdain dripping from his voice: "How convenient for you. Now I want to ask you, do you know Mrs. Bonnie Barton?"

Bob: "Yes, I do."

Mr. Cline: "And what is your relationship with her?"

Bob: "She is a good friend."

Mr. Cline: "Isn't it true that you have breakfast with her nearly every morning?"

Bob: "I have breakfast at her cafe most weekday mornings during the school year after I have taken her son to school."

63

THE TRIAL

Mr. Cline: "And do you have a key to Mrs. Barton's house?"

Bob: "Yes, I do. That was so Mrs. Barton could lock her house and leave her son, 'Little Buddy,' in bed for a couple of hours in the morning when she had to leave at around 5:30 AM to open the cafe. I would go by to take him to school each morning. Most mornings Buddy was dressed and waiting for me and would open the door and let me in, but there were times when I had to unlock the door and give Buddy a little help getting ready for school."

Mr. Cline: "Is it not true that Mrs. Barton and her small son are the only ones who live in that house?"

Bob: "Yes, that's true."

Mr. Cline: "Does anyone else have a key, or keys, to Mrs. Barton's home?"

Bob: "Not to my knowledge."

Mr. Cline: "Your Honor, I'm going to try to be discreet, but there are some questions pertinent to my case which I have to ask Mr. Morganton."

Judge Downs: "Go on, but remember you have been warned about rudeness and decorum."

Mr. Cline: "Mr. Morganton, you mentioned that on the night of July 4th Mrs. Morganton had fallen asleep on the couch, as you said she often did, and slept there through the night. I assume you are telling us that there are many nights when she did that. Am I correct?"

Bob: "Yes, she often did."

Mr. Cline: "Did she sometimes come to bed with you?"

Bob: "Oh yes, many nights."

Mr. Cline: "I think it is important that the court understand how normal the relationship between you and your wife had or had not been. Would you say that intimacy between you and your wife had been as strong in recent years as it was when you were first married?"

Mr. Reese: "Objection! This has nothing to do with this trial, and I think these questions are entirely inappropriate"

Mr. Cline: "Your Honor, I think they are necessary. It has to do with establishing state of mind in the accused, and has to do with motive."

Judge Downs: "I am also concerned about the direction this is going Mr. Cline. But, I do see where it has relevance, so you may continue. Mr. Morganton, answer the question."

Bob: "Kathy had not been well for several years now, and no, our intimacy had not been as strong as it once was; it had waned."

Mr. Cline: "It sounds to me like your relationship with your own wife may have become pretty platonic. I know as a minister you have counseled couples in this area many times, so I'm going to ask you: have you had a conjugal relationship with your wife during the past year?"

Bob: "Of course."

Mr. Cline: "Would you say it had been frequently, or infrequently?

Mr. Reese: "Objection! This is needless probing into unrelated matters."

Mr. Cline: "Your Honor, this is far from unrelated. Mr. Morganton's relationship with his wife is of extreme importance."

Judge Downs: "I don't like this either, but I have to concede it is pertinent to your case. You may continue."

Bob: "Compared to past years with her, I must say it had been infrequent."

Mr. Cline: "Would it be closer to 50 times in the past year, 25 times, 10 times or 5 times?"

Bob: "Probably 5 times."

Mr. Cline: "Is it not true that you have a life insurance policy worth $300,000 on your wife?'

Bob: "Yes, that is the case. We purchased it shortly after our marriage."

Mr. Cline: "And how much life insurance do you have?"

Bob: "$300,000"

Mr. Cline: "You are the bread winner for the family, are you not Mr. Morganton? If this is the case it seems unusual that you took out a policy on your wife as large as you have on yourself. In fact I know that at the time you purchased the policy your wife was unemployed. Can you explain that?"

Bob: "Our insurance agent told us that if we would take out the second policy, he would return half of his commission on that policy to us. This reduced our payments on that policy significantly, and even though the values of the policy are equal, our payments on hers was much less expensive. In addition to that the policy was a wise investment in view of Kathy's abilities. She was a very intelligent and multi-talented woman. She graduated from college as valedictorian of her class. She was not employed because more than anything else she wanted to be a wife and mother. If the time had come when she wanted to seek employment she would have had no problem finding a well paying job. She was worth many times more than $300,000."

Mr. Cline: "You do stand to collect $300,000 on your wife's insurance policy then?"

Bob: "Yes, that is correct."

Mr. Cline: "Thank you for your honesty. Your Honor, I have no further questions."

Judge Downs said, the court would be adjourned until the following morning.

When the court reconvened for the closing statements of the two attorneys, the statements on the part of the prosecuting attorney were even more sarcastic and aggressive than he had been before.

He began by saying, "I believe that Mr. Robert Morganton, although presenting himself as a man of God, is the quintessential hypocrite. If we consider the evidence in this case I see no other possibility than that he carefully planned what appeared to be an accident as a means of getting rid of his wife. By his deceit and treachery he committed premeditated vehicular homicide. Please recall from what we have heard:

Mr. Morganton, by his own admission, acknowledged that he does not consider himself worthy of the term "Reverend." He presents himself as an ordained minister, and yet he is not licensed by any denomination or synod or diocese or presbytery. He rather stands on the acknowledgment of one congregation to claim his credentials.

Beth Harper, the nurse in attendance when Mr. Morganton first regained consciousness after his accident, has testified that he did not seem surprised at the news of his wife's death, but rather quite quickly fell asleep.

Samuel Belton has testified that the impact on the car indicated that the automobile struck the tree at about the point of the right headlight. I believe that Mr. Morganton deliberately aimed the car at that tree in a way that he calculated would cause the greater damage on the passenger side of the car. I cannot think it was just coincidence that the car struck that huge oak about eight feet off the pavement when it is the only such large tree that close to the road for over ten miles.

Sheriff Henson has testified that the car struck the tree going at a speed at which air bags and fastened seat belts would almost certainly have saved the lives of passengers in the car, but would also almost certainly kill those who were not protected by air bags and seat belts. I think most people also know that the critical speed, the dividing line between survival and death in such incidences, is about

50 miles an hour, because that knowledge has been made known to the public. Certainly Mr. Morganton knew that, and calculated the speed at which he was driving when he struck that tree to make his survival almost certain and his wife's death almost certain.

There have been those who testified that Mrs. Morganton was always careful to fasten her seat belt. The only testimony that claimed she had become careless about this was from Karen Bailey. She was also the only corroborating witness of Mr. Morganton's claim that his presence in her room on the night of July 4th was totally innocent. I would remind you that she herself said she was barely aware of what was going on that night. And let us keep in mind that this is the woman with whom Mr. Morganton had been suspected of carrying on an illicit affair.

We must also remember that the only one Mr. Morganton said could verify the late night call to Dr. Marvin Moreland is Dr. Moreland, who is unavailable for comment. Also the only one he said could verify what work was done on his car before he left for the trip to Rockview is Elvin Taylor, who also is not available for cross examination. Can we really believe Mr. Morganton's stories when the only ones who could substantiate them are his paramour and two unavailable witnesses?

When first asked about the accident, Mr. Morganton said he could remember nothing about it. When questioned later, he then invented a story about swerving to miss an animal in the road. Later, aware now that he was under serious suspicion, his story evolved to say it was hog or a pig. However, investigation found no pigs raised anywhere within the surrounding two miles.

Mrs. Elizabeth Norton has testified that just before the Morganton's left Rockview on that Sunday afternoon she had heard

Mr. Morganton tell his wife that he was not going to put up with her any longer.

Ladies and gentlemen of the jury, we must understand that here is a man claiming to be a minister of the Gospel who has questionable credentials. This man opposed a casino in the city, and yet gambled when playing golf with his friends. His relationship with his wife had become quite platonic in recent years. He had his car serviced the morning before the accident, and he had threatened his wife as they were beginning their drive home that Sunday afternoon. In the accident the air bag on the passenger side of the car that had been serviced by a friend one day earlier, a friend who is unavailable for questioning, failed to operate. He lived in the same house with his sister-in-law, and also had her work with him for a time in the church office, which she gladly did without any monetary pay. He admits there had been a time when rumors were circulated about his relationship with her. He admits she is extremely attractive, and that he spent a night with her in her bedroom while his wife was soundly asleep a floor below, and yet expects us to believe there had been nothing untoward going on between them.

He also had a close relationship with an attractive widow who lived alone with her young son. Mr. Morganton had a key to her house, apparently the only one other than the ones Mrs. Barton had herself. He was free to enter and leave that house any time he wanted.

The facts would indicate that Mr. Morganton had carefully planned this so called "accident." He unbuckled his wife's seatbelt and deliberately drove into that lone tree, knowing that at the speed he was driving and with neither the air bag nor her seat belt to protect her, his wife would almost certainly be killed. He, on the other hand, with his seatbelt buckled and the driver side air bag functioning, would live. This is nothing short of premeditated, planned, murder. Discouraged by his platonic relationship with his wife, who seems to have become somewhat of an inconvenience to him, and motivated by his affair with his attractive sister-in-law and a close relationship with another attractive woman, and with a neat $300,000 in insurance which Mr. Morganton stood to collect at his wife's death, this man transformed his automobile into a lethal weapon and brutally planned and carried out the murder of his wife. In the light of such obvious planning for this so-called "accident," justice demands nothing less than a verdict of first degree murder."

In his closing remarks in defense of Bob, Mr. Reese pointed out inaccuracies in Mr. Cline's summation. He reminded the jury that heavy medication, shock, or several other factors could account for nurse Beth Harper's perception that Bob had not shown surprise or strong emotional reaction upon learning of his wife's death.

He also pointed out that there are thousands of congregations served by preachers whose ordination was by a local congregation rather than an overseeing ecclesiastical hierarchy. He stated that the church in which he was a member was served by a minister whose ordination had been by a local congregation. He asked, "Who could best determine the qualifications and character necessary for one to be ordained; the congregation who has observed his life and service through the years, or a removed ecclesiastical authority which had no opportunity for up close observation of the man?" He stated that the preacher at the church where he attended, like Bob, did not accept the title "Reverend."

Mr. Reese further pointed out that recovery of memory after an accident that has caused a concussion was often a slow process, and it was not unusual for the patient to be at first unable to recall some details that later he could clearly remember.

He reminded the jury that Bob had admitted the group he had played golf with paid a penny a hole for the holes they lost, but challenged Mr. Cline's insinuation that such was serious gambling.

He corrected Mr. Cline's word choice in two instances. He had not "threatened" Kathy before they left the Rockview church, but had said he would no longer put up with her negativism. Also, Bob had agreed that Karen Bailey was "attractive" but had not said "extremely attractive."

He closed his remarks by saying "Here is a man who in recent days has been submitted to grossly unfair and damaging accusations. Yet those who have known him best since his coming to this community a few years ago know him as a sincere and honest man. In spite of his wife's illness in the past couple of years he continued to care for her with great tenderness and love. The rumors about unfaithfulness to her are completely without foundation. Mr. Cline has developed a persuasive scenario, but I am sure you will have the wisdom to see it is built wholly on circumstantial evidence, and will return the only just decision: **Not guilty**."

While the jury was deliberating, Bob asked Ronald Reese how he felt the decision might go. He answered, "Arthur Cline has done a masterful job in researching many things about the accident and what went before it. However, his case is totally circumstantial, and it is unusual for a jury to return a guilty verdict in a murder trial on circumstantial evidence. However, I really wish that Dr. Moreland and Elvin Taylor had been here to testify. We also would have been much better off if the police had located a pig farm somewhere in the vicinity. We can only pray that the jury comes to the right decision."

The jury was not long in deliberation. When it was announced that a decision had been reached, Ronald Reese said, "Bob, that's usually not good. This quick a decision is most often a guilty verdict."

THE TRIAL

And sure enough, it was. The jury foreman announced they had come to a decision that the defendant was guilty of first degree murder. The state had mandated that the sentence for first degree murder was either the death penalty, or life imprisonment. Judge Herald Downs sentenced Bob to life imprisonment, with parole possible in thirty years.

What followed in the courtroom was unprecedented. Bonnie Barton and Karen Bailey were embracing and weeping on each other's shoulder. The elders of the church, Roger Jones, John Black, Clarence White, and Jerry Johnson, with their wives, as well as Denver Newton, the Hillsborough preacher, came to the front where Bob and Ronald Reese had been seated at the defense table. They spontaneously surrounded that table in a circle.

Bonnie Barton and Karen Bailey came to join them. Standing shoulder to shoulder they each of them had put their arms around the shoulder of those on either side. Tears were flowing. Denver Newton suggested they pray, and he led in prayer: "Father, we know you are a just and holy God. It is our desire to see justice done. But Father, down deep inside we believe that an innocent man has been condemned. Only you, our God, know the full truth in all of this, and we pray and we know that ultimately your justice will prevail. We pray your presence with our dear brother who will now be incarcerated. Please Father, be with him and bless him even as you have always blessed your children through every trial. We pray this in the name of Your Son, who so sacrificially suffered for all of us. Amen." One policeman attending Bob had not rushed to intercede or stop this spontaneous prayer session. He instead watched with a sense of perplexity and admiration.

Bob Morganton then spoke. "Dear ones, please hold firm your faith, and don't despair now. I am innocent and unjustly condemned, but I remind you Scripture says 'In nothing be anxious, but in everything by prayer and supplication with thanksgiving let your requests be made known unto God, and the peace of God which passes all understanding shall guard your hearts and your thoughts in Christ Jesus.(7) Please remember that after Joseph had been betrayed by his own brothers, sold into slavery, falsely accused and imprisoned, he was able to look back on it all and see it was all in the plan of God to save lives.(8) And don't forget that it was from prison that Paul wrote that the things that had happened to him had resulted in progress for the Gospel. (9) I hope that you good people haven't forgotten what I have preached to you for several years now from Romans 8:28 'We know that to them that love God (they joined him and finished in unison) all things work together for good.' Bob went on 'and remember the rest of that verse, *them that are called according to His purpose.*' Please don't forget that God has a purpose in all of our lives; in mine now as a prisoner and in each one of yours as you live each day. He will bless us as we continue to seek to fulfill His purpose."

It was Karen with her soft, melodious voice who began the hymn, but Denver Newton with his strong voice, and then all the others joined in "Praise God from whom all blessings flow, Praise Him all creatures here below. Praise Him above, ye heavenly hosts, Praise Father, Son and Holy Ghost."

Judge Downs had tarried in the courtroom, observing all this, as had the local newspaper editor, Orville Nelson, who had been in court for almost all of the trial. Orville looked at the judge and said, "I have never seen anything like that in a courtroom."

Judge Downs said, "Neither have I, not in all my experience." The courtroom emptied, and Bob Morganton was led out and transported to the state penitentiary, seventy miles away.

THE GOSPEL NOT BOUND

After the trial Orville Nelson wrote an editorial in the <u>Conner's Crossing Crier</u> stating his disappointment that the jury had convicted Robert Morganton on purely circumstantial evidence. He acknowledged that Bob's claim to having swerved in an effort to avoid hitting a pig when no pigs could be found in the area, and that the air bag failed just after the car had been serviced by Bob's friend were damaging bits of evidence, but still he was not comfortable with a first degree murder conviction on circumstantial evidence. However, other newspapers throughout the area blazed headlines like, "**MINISTER GUILTY OF FIRST DEGREE MURDER.**"

The Lord did not forget His servant while he was in prison. Neither did the Lord's family. The elders of the church decided that each month one of them would take his wife and drive the seventy miles to the state penitentiary to visit Bob. The first few times only one person at a time was allowed into a visitation area where he would sit and talk by phone to Bob who sat on the other side of a window. Later, however, they allowed Bob and other prisoners to come into a larger room where two guards watched as Bob could visit with the elder and his wife. Bob greatly appreciated their visits, and when he told them so they would answer, "Bob, you remember what Jesus said in Matthew 25 about visiting those in prison. Even so, we are not doing this only because of duty and to be accepted on

Judgment Day, but we miss you back in Conner's Crossing, and enjoy coming to visit with you." Their visits enabled Bob to keep up with things at the New Haven church in Conner's Crossing and he was glad to hear they had called Daniel Melton, whom Bob had known during his seminary days, to be their preacher and that, although there had been some drop in attendance when Bob left, that they were now beginning to grow again, and that Brother Melton fit their needs well and was appreciated and supported by the congregation.

One time on visitation day Clyde and Elizabeth Norton, from the Rockview church, came to visit Bob. Mrs. Norton described how sorry she was that she had testified at the trial. She said, "Brother Morganton, I don't know who overheard us during that conversation at your car that Sunday afternoon. Arthur Cline came to Rockview and evidently talked to many people trying to find something to use against you. Someone other than me heard that remark you made about Kathy's negative attitude, and evidently told Mr. Cline. He came to me and had a subpoena ordering me to appear in court as a witness. I hated to do that, and if I had any other choice, I would not have gone."

Bob answered, "Elizabeth, I understand, and certainly do not hold it against you. You obeyed the law, you answered honestly, and I am sure you did what God would have you to do. It's a little hard to understand just now, but I am still confident that God is going to use all this to His glory."

One visitor who surprised Bob was Orville Nelson, the editor of the <u>Conner's Crossing Crier</u>. He began to visit Bob about once a month, and told him that he wanted to begin a series, a feature to run once every three months, about life in a state penitentiary. Bob had read Orville's editorial about his disappointment with a conviction only on circumstantial evidence and thanked him for it.

Bob enjoyed his monthly visits with Orville. He found him to be honest and astute in his research and reporting.

Walter Grey was the prison chaplain and Bob liked him from the first day they met. He was not employed by the prison, but came in as a volunteer to conduct Sunday afternoon worship services in the prison. In addition, he was allowed to meet after the weekly service with any of the inmates who wanted to sit with him for a question and answer period. This afforded further teaching opportunities for the chaplain, and for some counseling with inmates who may desire it. He had also secured a Bible study course with several of the inmates. He was a large man, about 6 foot 3 and 240 pounds. Walter was athletic, and kept himself in good shape. He was so well proportioned that one did not notice, unless standing beside him, how large he was. In spite of his size and age, he was agile and moved quickly. He was retired from the military service, and the inmates referred to him as Chaplain Grey, and sometimes as "the Lieutenant." He had not been a chaplain in the military, but had served as a chaplain's assistant. He walked with a slight limp which didn't seem to hamper him as he moved about the prison. Perhaps the limp was from being wounded in the military. Bob didn't ask him, and the chaplain seemed hesitant to talk about his military experience.

Bob attended each time there were worship services in the prison. The large dining/visitation room was transformed into a worship area for those services. Bob appreciated the preaching and teaching of Chaplain Grey. His messages were filled with Scripture, and he seemed to have an unusual knack of applying the texts to the needs of the prisoners.

Bob chatted informally with the chaplain each time he had opportunity. The chaplain soon learned of Bob's former life in the ministry, and of the fact that he was sentenced to a life term for murder. The chaplain one day said to Bob, "Mr. Morganton, I know that 90 percent of these inmates claim they were sentenced even though innocent of the charges. But I believe you. I think that I am a good enough judge of character to have concluded rightly that you could not be guilty of the charges against you. Bob, I would like to ask you if you would assist me in my ministry here."

The possibility excited Bob. When he asked what it would entail the chaplain told him that he would like for Bob to work with the inmates who were taking the Bible courses, to encourage and tutor them when needed. He said that he had noticed Bob had a pleasant singing voice, and that he knew the choruses and hymns they sang. He asked him if he would lead singing during the worship times. Bob remarked that he had never been a song leader, but he had been singing in church since he was a toddler, and agreed to give it a try.

This worked well, and a few weeks later chaplain Grey asked, "Bob, have you ever played guitar?" Bob said he had never played any musical instrument, and the chaplain said, "I believe you could learn guitar quite easily, and although you have done well leading singing without any instrumental accompaniment, I believe a guitar might improve our worship. I can get you a guitar, and I think I can talk to the prison personnel and get permission for it to be kept here, and for you to be allowed to practice and learn to play it."

Chaplain Grey had earned the respect of the prison guards and administration to a degree that caused them to immediately grant his request. The next week the chaplain brought the guitar, and Bob began to practice. He was a fast learner, and soon was accomplished enough to play for the chapel services. Chaplain Grey was right- -this did improve the singing during their worship.

After some time, Chaplain Grey asked Bob if he would preach for him on occasions. He said he would like to be able to give some time on Sunday afternoons to projects at the church where he was a member, and also to spend a bit more time with his own family. Bob agreed, and began preaching to the inmates about once a month.

Norman Wilson was the prison guard who weekly accompanied the inmates to the worship services and stood guard while the services were being conducted. He was a short, stocky, evidently strong man with a round jovial face. One day as the services were being concluded he told Bob he would like to speak with him for a few moments. He accompanied Bob to his cell and said, much like the chaplain had said, "Bob, nearly everyone in this place claims innocence, even though they are obviously guilty. However there's something about you that makes me believe there is no way you could have murdered your wife. I have observed you, not only as you have led the worship services sometimes, but all the rest of the time you have been here. There is a quality about you that speaks of integrity. You have said some things in chapel that make me want to tell you of my situation, and ask if you could help me."

"Go on," Bob said.

Officer Wilson continued: "My wife and I have had a good marriage, and are basically happy. However, in recent months things have developed that have me deeply concerned. Our son is about to finish middle school and begin high school, and frankly we are concerned about some of the things we're seeing in him now. He has lost all interest in school, and although before he always was a good student, presently his grades are dropping sharply. He says he hates school, and wants to quit school and get a job as soon as he can. He is beginning to keep company with some other kids who trouble us; we suspect that some of them are using drugs. We have tried to discourage him from associating with them, but he gets defensive and sometimes almost belligerent when we bring it up. This has caused some friction between my wife and me. I am trying to keep our son from getting into trouble, but my wife thinks I am too suspicious and too hard on him. I have tended to want to curtail his activities, but she believes I am too restrictive with him. I haven't figured out what to do a about it."

Bob asked, "Officer Wilson, do you and your family have any church relationship, or more importantly, do you feel you have a relationship with Jesus Christ?" Officer Wilson responded: "I know it might not be protocol, but I want you to call me Norm, and drop the Officer title."

Bob replied, "Well, thank you Norm. That does seem more natural, and just call me Bob."

Norman then said, "But to answer your question; Yes, we are members of a church. When I was young I went to Sunday school regularly, and have a chain of perfect attendance pins to show it. However, even though my parents attended church spasmodically, they wanted me to attend Sunday school even when they didn't go, and sometimes would take me to the church building and drop me off. As I grew older I concluded that church was for kids, and until I married I stopped going almost altogether. My wife, however, insisted that we have a church wedding, and after we were married we joined that church, and have attended sometimes, perhaps an average of about once a month."

Bob told Norman: "Norm, I am convinced that, no matter what the situation, God's plan is always best. And He does have, and in fact has made known, His plan for a happy home. He tells us that the father is to be the spiritual head of the household, and that the wife is to honor his leadership. He lays an even heavier responsibility on the husband than on the wife. While he tells the wife to be submissive to her husband, he tells the husband to love his wife like Christ loved the church. This is a redemptive, sacrificial love. It means the husband should be willing to lay down his life for his wife. And Norm, I am convinced that your wife needs to see that kind of love manifest in your relationship to her. While you are to assume leadership in the home, never let your wife doubt your love for her. Be a leader, but not a dictator. Let your love for your wife be evident to your son. It has often been said 'the greatest thing a father can do for his children is to love their mother.' This whole relationship is to be in submission to Christ. In the Christian home the father cannot expect the submission of the family to his leadership unless he is fully submissive to Christ."

Bob went on: "Norm, all this is in Ephesians chapter 5 verses 21-33. Then in the beginning of Chapter 6 Paul carries on his instructions for the Christian home. He tells the children to obey their parents in the Lord. The fathers are not to provoke their children to wrath, but are to nurture them in the Lord. When kids see parents who acknowledge a God who is sovereign over their lives and who are obedient to Him, parents who love one another from the very depth of their being, those children are more inclined to honor and obey their parents. However, Norm, you cannot expect your family to honor your leadership unless you are willing to be completely submissive to the will of God in your own life. You and your wife need to agree on how strict or lenient you are going to be with your son. You need to establish rules on which the two of you concur, and then make them clear to your son. Make it plain to him that the two of you are in agreement and are in harmony on enforcing them.

Officer Wilson was listening with an interest that surprised him, so Bob went on. "Norman, I want you to do two things. First get active again, not as a spectator, but as a participant in the church where you are a member. Attend every time you can. I would suggest that when you are actively involved again you go to the leadership of that church and volunteer to serve. I think it might be good, in fact, if you offered to become a youth sponsor. It would be great if you could sponsor a group the age of your own son. Get close with these kids, go with them on outings, invite them into your home and hopefully your own son will begin to appreciate spending time and "hanging out" with young people whose influence on him would be much healthier than that of his present companions."

Bob was aware that he still had Norm's rapt attention, so he continued. "Norm, the next thing you ought to do is bring Christ into your home in a significant way. Establish a time of Bible reading and prayer with your wife and son. I have shared Ephesians 5:21-6:4 with you today. To let your wife and son know that what you are doing is not simply by your own authority, but by the authority of the Lord. I would suggest that as a family you read those verses together at least three times a week."

Norman had listened intently through all that Bob had said but now he looked a bit overwhelmed. He sat with his head down, and seemed to be in deep thought. Bob said to him, "Maybe I've heaped too much on you in one conversation, Norm. However, I would like for us to pray together before we end this." Norman raised his eyes with a look of surprise and a bit of fear. "Oh brother Bob," he said. "It's been a long time since I've prayed. I don't believe I could do that." "Well," Bob said as he gripped Norm's hand, "that's all right. Just bow your head with me and I'll lead our prayer." Norm looked at Bob rather sheepishly, but nodded yes, and bowed his head. Bob thanked the Lord for Norman's desire to seek for answers from God, for the opportunity this had afforded him to share God's Word with him, and then prayed that God would strengthen Norm as he sought to lead his family in a closer walk with the Lord.

Attendance at the prison chapel service was entirely voluntary. No one was coerced to attend. Most of the men who came seemed to enjoy it, perhaps because it provided a break from their otherwise boring routine. Some probably came thinking it would impress the prison administration, and might enhance their chances when reviews for parole came up. Some joined in the services with gusto, singing wholeheartedly, listening to the sermons with a genuine interest and warmly chatting with other inmates. One young man, however, soon caught Bob's attention. It appeared as though he didn't want to be there, but yet he continued to come regularly. Bob could not help wondering why he continued to attend regularly, hardly ever missing one of the services. Yet he came in sullenly, sat quietly through most of the song services, although on rare occasions he would join in the singing. He seemed indifferent to the sermon or lesson of the day. He was a very young man, Bob guessed about twenty years old. After the services he would usually leave quickly with little conversation with the other men. Bob puzzled over this young inmate - why would he keep attending when it seemed to mean so little to him? As Bob watched him for a few weeks, he thought he could detect a glimmer of interest developing in him. He began to join in more of the singing, and listened with a bit more interest to the preaching. Bob concluded that he must be looking for something. He also decided that he would try to make his acquaintance and see if he could determine how he might help him. He noted that the young man had very little contact with the other prisoners. He was a real loner. He kept to himself and whatever feeling he may have had never showed.

One day Bob went and sat with this inmate during lunch in the dining room. He tried to involve him in conversation but the young man usually responded with a one word answer, or just a nod of the head. He had learned that the man's name was Glen, and Bob said to him, "Glen, my name is Bob Morganton," hoping that the man would respond telling his last name. Instead he simply replied, "I know that. My name is Glen." Try as he might, he could not seem to penetrate Glen's shell. Bob did tell Glen that he appreciated his regular attendance at chapel, and hoped he found it helpful. After several awkward attempts at conversation, as they were finishing their lunch, Bob, mustering as much sincerity as he could said, "Glen, I've enjoyed having lunch with you, and hope we might get together again soon." Glen said "Thank you," picked up his tray and returned it to the dishwashing area.

Glen was on Bob's mind all night long. He prayed that the Lord would somehow open the heart of Glen so he could have a deeper conversation with him. He thought that perhaps Glen's withdrawn nature was due to shyness, but he could not help but feel there was something deeper, something that troubled this man even more than the multitude of prisoners about him were troubled.

Perhaps it was an answer to his prayer, but it certainly was a surprise to Bob that the next day Glen brought his lunch to Bob's table and sat with him again. Bob secretly breathed a prayer of thanksgiving, and emboldened by the fact that Glen had come to him decided to probe a bit into Glen's thoughts. This time rather than just saying he hoped Glen was gaining something from the chapel services, he asked, "Glen, as I said yesterday I am always glad to have you in our worship services. I need to know something. Do you find our services helpful to you personally?" Glen responded "Well, I think so. Worship is kind of new to me."

Bob pushed a bit further: "Glen, I have noticed that in recent weeks you have been a bit more involved in the chapel services, but for a long time I was concerned; you seemed indifferent to everything about the chapel service." Glen replied, "Well, as I said, attending any kind of worship is pretty new to me. However, I must admit the preaching of Chaplain Grey and your preaching and teaching have made me think about things I had never thought of before."

"What do you mean?" queried Bob. "What new thoughts have you had since you've been listening to Bible preaching and teaching?"

Glen said, "Things about grace and forgiveness. I always thought that God set some pretty high standards for us, and that if we fell below them - too bad, we were out of luck. But I hear you and Chaplain Grey talk about a God who forgives, a God of love who really has no desire to condemn anyone. I only wish I could hope for such forgiveness."

Bob assured him he could have such hope, but that perhaps there were things he wasn't willing to really lay before God, to fully confess. But Glen answered, "Well, I've already been found guilty and incarcerated, so I can't see where further confession would help anything. Besides, the things I've done even God couldn't forgive no matter how many times I confessed them. I have heard of the unpardonable sin, and I don't understand what that is, but I think I must have committed it."

Bob told him that the very fact he desired forgiveness, and his willingness to talk about it was evidence that he had not committed the unpardonable sin. He wanted Glen to go on, but Glen began to withdraw again, and then said, "Well, I've said too much already. I don't want to talk about it anymore."

Bob said, "I'm sorry about that, Glen. You really need to deal with this matter, and turn it over to God. I want you to know I sincerely want to talk with you more about it. I promise you, God does want to forgive you."

Glen left, and Bob's heart sank. He silently prayed that God would soon open the door for further contacts with Glen.

To Bob's deep disappointment, Glen was not at the chapel service the next Sunday afternoon, and seemed to be avoiding Bob in the dining hall. Bob continued praying for Glen, and watchfully hoped for another opportunity to witness to Glen.

To Bob's delight, Glen was present at the chapel worship service the following Sunday. After Bob had concluded leading the song service, he slipped into the chair beside Glen. When the service had ended he said to Glen: "Glen, I don't know what you have been convicted of, but I do know that I am in here convicted of murder, yet God has continued to bless my life and let me serve Him. I can't help but believe, no matter what you've done, that God wants to forgive you and bless your life."

Glen looked at Bob with astonishment. "But," he said, "I don't believe you're guilty, and neither do most of the men in this prison. I've done something worse than murder, and not only am I guilty as charged, but I've done things beyond even what I have already been charged and convicted for....things that even my accusers do not know."

Bob replied, "But you and I both know that God knows. Glen, His mercy is beyond our comprehension. You are carrying a burden of guilt that God wants to remove from you. Believe me, He can do that. Please let me help you with that."

Tears began to well up in Glen's eyes. It was a break-through, the first time when there had been even the slightest display of emotion on the part of Glen.

Trying to regain his composure, Glen said: "I have been convicted of child abuse and rape. Not only have I been convicted, but I am guilty." Through the sobs, he went on "I violated my own niece when she was only 13 years old. Can anything be more unforgivable than that?"

Bob responded, "Glen, the apostle John, Jesus' beloved apostle, writes in I John 1:7 that the blood of Jesus is able to cleanse us from ALL sin. That means ALL Glen; there is nothing for which God cannot forgive us if we genuinely believe and sincerely repent."

"But" Glen then said. "There is more. Not only did I rape my niece, my brother's daughter, but I did the same thing to my nephew, my sister's son. He was 11 years old. There was no charge brought against me for that, probably because after the first episode with him, he became a willing partner and we carried on a secret relationship until I was sent to prison. Certainly this is beyond the scope of God's forgiveness." Glen was now weeping openly, and tears were also flowing from Bob's eyes. He said, "Glen, ALL sin means ALL sin. However, there is a condition to that promise in I John 1:7. It says 'if we walk in the light'. You have been in darkness, but perhaps one of the reasons God has allowed me to be in this prison and to meet you, is to help you see and walk in the light of God."

The announcement was made that it was time for the dining hall, which was used for the chapel service, to be vacated. The prisoners were ordered to return to their cells. Before they left, Glen and Bob embraced, and Bob said, "Glen, we need to continue this conversation. God is granting repentance to you, and we must follow up and let Him complete the work He is doing in your life."

As Glen and Bob met regularly in the following days Glen confessed to him that he had battled, and continued to battle, with unwholesome lust. The times he had succumbed to it had resulted in the prison term he was now enduring. However, he admitted that it was still a constant battle, and that although there were many men around him in the prison he had not been strongly attracted to them. He said this was probably because all the other men in the prison were older than he was, and that his temptations seemed to be stronger when he was with younger boys or girls. He confessed to Bob that he still often fantasized about young boys and girls. One day with a sense of desperation he said "And there doesn't seem to be anything I can do about it. I have resolved many times to put these things out of my mind, but the temptation keeps coming back stronger and stronger."

Bob said, "Glen, this is something you will never be able to lick on your own. What you need is a heart transplant."

"What in the world do you mean Bob?" Glen said. "There's nothing wrong with my heart. All my medical check ups have come back good."

"What I mean," Bob answered, "is that you are trying to change things, even your thought patterns, by your own resolve and self reformation. In his great prayer of repentance David prayed in Psalm 51:10 'Create in me a clean heart, O God, and renew a right spirit within me.' Remember, David had been guilty of adultery and murder, and he realized that God had to do a work of re-creation within him. He knew he couldn't make the changes he needed without God making him new from the inside out. Jesus said an entire new birth was necessary. That's why Paul wrote in II Corinthians 5:17 "If any man is in Christ, he is a new creature.""

The dining hall was a rather austere place for the chapel worship services. However, when the services were to be held on Sunday afternoons there was a large box about seven feet long that was moved from one of the corners of the room to front and center in the dining hall. This box really was the Communion Table for observing the Lord's Supper. On the front of it was inscribed, "IN REMEMBRANCE OF ME." It had a one piece lid that could be removed, and the inside of the box was actually a baptistry. It could be filled with water and drained by a hose.(10) For the worship service a short speaker's lectern was placed on top of this table. Not long after Bob had begun his conversations with Glen, one of the inmates was baptized. Glen watched this with deep interest, and came to Bob and said, "I heard Chaplain Grey say that he was baptizing that man into Christ for the remission of sin, and for the gift of the Holy Spirit. Will you explain that to me, and anything else about baptism?"

"Gladly," Bob answered. "What Chaplain Grey said is taken directly from Scripture, from Acts 2:38. It was in answer to the question thousands had asked just after they had learned that the one for whose crucifixion they had cried out for just a few weeks earlier was really Christ, God's anointed. This cut them to the heart, and they cried out asking what to do. Peter told them to repent and be baptized into the name of Christ and they would receive both the forgiveness of their sin, and the gift of the Holy Spirit."

"But Mr. Morganton," said Glen, "You told me a few days ago that I needed the help of the Holy Spirit to whip this lust in my heart. I have been praying for that, and although that lust is not all gone, I believe something has been helping me. At least I have a greater hatred for the things I have done, I know this evil intent in my heart is wrong, even though I haven't made much progress in overcoming it."

Bob replied, "John 16:8 tells us that the Holy Spirit would convict the world of sin. You have been feeling that conviction. Acts 5:32 lets us see that God gives the Holy Spirit to those who obey him. What you heard Chaplain Grey say to that inmate was because he was obeying the Lord in baptism, and thus the Holy Spirit would now personally come into his life. When He does, He provides many, many blessings. Among other things, Romans Chapter 8 informs us that the Holy Spirit sets us free from the law of sin and death, He gives us moral strength to overcome temptations, He helps us keep our minds focused on things of God, He helps us control our sinful nature, He helps us pray, He intercedes for us even when we don't know how we ought to pray, and by His power He will also raise us from the dead."

Glen had been listening with a wide-eyed attention; almost astonishment. "That's awesome," he said.

"Our God is an awesome God," Bob replied.

"I'm beginning to see that," said Glen. "Mr. Morganton, as you tell me more about Him, I can understand how you have been able to maintain such a positive attitude even though a prisoner. What you have taught me so far has helped me immensely, and I want to know more."

"Let me tell you more then about what happens when one is baptized," said Bob. "Galatians 3:27 tells us that it is at that point that we come into Christ, that we actually clothe ourselves with Him. Romans 6:3 tells us that when we are baptized into Him we are baptized into His death. It was at His death, in the shedding of His blood, that the price was paid for our sins. Therefore, we need to contact Him at the point of His death for His atoning power, the cleansing of our sins, to take place. In the following verses Paul tells us that as when we are immersed in water in baptism we are buried with Him, and like He came forth from the grave this brings to us the hope of our resurrection with Him. In verse 4 of this chapter he tells us that it is when this has occurred that we have a new life. Remember that we must be born again to have eternal life, and Scripture pictures baptism as the time we die to the old life, and have new life in Christ, we experience a new birth. This is not a work which we do that merits salvation, it is rather submission to the Word and authority of God and is dependent upon His work. This is why Paul wrote to Titus in chapter 3, verse 5, 'He saved us not because of righteous things we have done, but because of His mercy He saved us through the washing of rebirth and renewal by the Holy Spirit.' This is so much like what Jesus said in John 3:5 'unless a man is born of the water and the Spirit he cannot enter the kingdom of God.' What Jesus called birth of the water and the Spirit Paul calls washing of rebirth and renewal of the Holy Spirit. Paul also makes it clear that this is not a work of righteousness which we did ourselves, but faith in what God promises He will do when he writes in Colossians 2:12, 'having been buried with Him in baptism and raised with Him through your faith in the power of God who raised Him from the dead.'"

"So you see, Glen, we can try forever to save ourselves by our own good works, but we can never do that. We must yield ourselves to God's power, believe His promise, obey Him in being united with Christ in the likeness of His death in baptism, and then rise to walk in a new life. Even Saul of Tarsus, whom we know as the apostle Paul experienced this, for Acts 22:16 tells us that when Ananias, a Christian in Damascus, had come to Saul and restored his sight which he had lost three days earlier when the Lord had appeared to him, Ananias said to him 'now what are you waiting for, get up, be baptized and wash your sins away, calling on His name.' In I Peter 3:20, 21 we learn that just as Noah was saved when he obeyed God and built the ark, so does our obedience in baptism save us now."

"Wow," said Glen. "If in baptism a person puts on Christ, unites with His death, has his sins washed away and is given the gift of the Holy Spirit and so is saved, why can't I be baptized?"

"You can," answered Bob. "but you must do it in complete faith in Christ. If it is just a mechanical act, just a ritual for you, it will mean nothing. But if you do it in absolute submission to the authority of Christ who commanded it, and if you believe without reservation that Jesus is Christ the Son of the Living God, you may. Such faith, realizing that God loved you enough to send His Son into the world to die for you, and knowing that God's Son also loved you enough to die in the horrible way that He did should cause you to love God and Christ enough to be dissatisfied until you respond to that love in obedience to God. I believe in what I have seen in you, your tears of remorse a few days ago, in the eagerness you have shown to know what God's Word says, you have displayed genuine repentance and a sincere desire to make Christ the Lord of your life. Can you honestly say from the depth of your being that you do believe that Jesus is the Christ, God's Son and that you love Him?"

Tears began to flow again as Glen answered, "Yes, I believe that. I surely do."

The following day was Sunday, and after the sermon had ended, the small lectern was removed from the Communion table. Then the lid was removed, opening up the baptismal pool the table contained. Chaplain Grey then immersed Glen in the water that filled the large area inside the table. When Glen came out of the water, that face that had often looked so sullen and anxious shined with a smile that seemed to light up the whole room.

And that smile didn't fade. Everyone in the prison was struck by the change that had taken place in Glen's attitude. Previously the most withdrawn and reclusive inmate in the prison had become the most vibrant and outgoing. His incarceration didn't seem to trouble him at all. And Glen could not contain the new enthusiasm that filled him. He wanted to share with everyone the marvelous relief he had experienced. He enrolled in the Bible study series, and studied it with zeal. As he got deeper into it his interest only increased, and he began to enlist others in the prison to sign up. There had been about 15 men taking the course, but with Glen's enthusiastic recruiting taking place, that number soon grew to nearly fifty.(11)

Glen's influence also had a great effect on the chapel services. Noting the changes that had taken place in Glen, and hearing his testimony about how it had happened, more and more of the inmates started attending. Bob watched all this with gratitude and prayed, "Lord thank you for bringing me here. I see now how this is working out for your glory and my good."

Bob had been impressed at the singing voice of one of the regular chapel attendees. He kept hearing a rich tenor voice contributing to the harmony of the song service. Sometimes as Bob was leading he would stop singing and listen to the voices of the men. As he did he became aware that there was also a full and mellow bass voice among the men. He took note of who these men were, and went to them and asked if they would be interested in forming a prison quartet. Both expressed immediate interest. He talked with Chaplain Grey, whom Bob had heard singing a harmony part during the song service, and asked him if he could sing baritone. Walter said that he had on occasions and Bob suggested they start a prison quartet. These began practicing together, and soon were singing at many of the chapel services.

Orville Nelson, the editor of the Conner's Crossing Crier, had continued to visit Bob, and hearing what had been happening at the chapel services, he began coming on weekends, and staying long enough to attend the chapel services. He was greatly impressed, and his quarterly article about life inside a prison began to feature what was going on with the chapel services and Bible studies. He titled one large article "**Revival In The State Penitentiary.**" This article was not only read with deep interest by the people in the Conner's

Crossing community, but other newspapers in the area picked it up, and it soon had almost state-wide circulation. Again Bob Morganton prayed, "Lord, thank you for working out your marvelous purpose in things that first seemed to be puzzling and meaningless to me."

One day guard Norman Wilson came again to Bob's cell to talk with him. He said, "Bob, I've noticed the baptisms at chapel lately. I have never been immersed, and when I think of the picture that is of complete submission to Christ, even involving our physical body being surrendered to Him, and of the beautiful picture it is of the death, burial and resurrection of Christ, I have decided I want to be immersed." It was rather a shock to the prisoners on one of the Sundays shortly thereafter to see one of their guards immersed in the baptistry by the prison chaplain.

Bob again prayed, "Thank you Heavenly Father, for working all things together for those who love you."

Orville Nelson continued to carry news of the prison chapel. When churches in the area read of the prison quartet they began to inquire of the prison administration if these men could be allowed to come and sing in their churches, or in other religious gatherings. With one of the quartet being the prison chaplain, not an inmate, the administration agreed that by sending one guard with them this could be done. Norman Wilson quickly volunteered to be that guard, and to go with the quartet on his own time, not expecting to receive any salary for the time he was with them. On those occasions Norman would bring his wife and son with him. The quartet had by now become quite accomplished. Upon hearing that they were going to be invited to sing outside the prison they decided they should have a name. Bob pointed out to them that the root word for "angel" in the Bible means messenger. They decided to take the Greek word for angel in the plural, Angeloi, as a part of their name. They became known, and quite quickly well known, as the Inmate Angeloi quartet, the inmate messengers quartet. There were numerous requests for them, and soon they were traveling almost every week, usually on a Saturday evening, to sing in the area. Again Bob took note, and thanked God for the amazing ways the years of his incarceration were working out for the glory of God and bringing great joy to his life. He commented to Chaplain Grey, "Now I see more clearly why Paul, while a prisoner, wrote to Timothy, 'the Word of God is not imprisoned.'"

EVIDENCE RE-EXAMINED

As Orville Nelson had covered the stories of life in the state penitentiary he had become more and more convinced of Robert Morganton's innocence, and more and more concerned about the evidence that had led to his conviction. With the mind of an honest reporter, he began his own research. He learned some things that he brought to the State Attorney's office, with a request that the evidence that had led to Morganton's conviction be re-examined. Mr. Nelson wanted to tell Bob of his findings, but he did not do that because of concern that he might give Bob hope that would not come to fruition. However, the State Attorney was carefully examining the things that Orville Nelson had brought to him and followed up with some research of his own.

One day the warden of the penitentiary came to Bob's cell. He said, "Mr. Morganton, some things have come to light that have caused the state to re-open your case. You, and some witnesses, are going to appear before the State Attorney and your case is going to be reconsidered. During this time you will be under constant guard, and will be returned to prison each night."

This news surprised Bob. In fact, it caused a bit of perplexity in him. He had come to believe that God had put him prison for a very definite purpose, and that purpose was being fulfilled in wonderful and amazing ways. He wondered, if he should be released, how God would use him more effectively outside of prison than He had used him in prison.

When Bob appeared before the State Attorney and a panel of three men and two women who were to reconsider his case, Orville Nelson was also there. He presented the things he had learned during his research about Bob's trial.

Orville Nelson had learned that the car model, and the models for two years before and one year after the model that Bob had driven, had been recalled. It had been learned that on 23% of these models the air bags had malfunctioned. Most of the failures had been on the front seat passenger side. Orville presented documentation from the car manufacturer to verify his claims.

A state trooper was also there to report other things Orville Nelson had discovered. He reported that on that less traveled route where the Morganton's accident had occurred there had been several incidents reported where cars had swerved off the road to avoid hitting wild boars. The trooper had dates these incidents had taken place. One of them had been previous to the Morganton accident, but several had been shortly afterward.

Orville Nelson presented a document showing that the state Fish and Game Commission had opened a hunting season on wild boar in the county because of the increasing number of wild pigs and hogs that had been spotted. Such evidence made Bob's claim that he had swerved to avoid hitting a pig much more credible.

Orville then presented to the panel a notarized affidavit which Elvin Taylor, who was still in the Navy, had sent stating that on the day he had serviced Bob's car he had changed spark plugs, changed the oil, rotated the tires and did a tune up, but had not touched the air bag system.

Dr. Marvin Moreland was also there to testify. He verified the fact that on the night of July 4th he had received a phone call from Bob Morganton, and the conversation about Karen's illness, as Bob and Karen had born witness in court, was accurate. He had advised Bob to stay near Karen and monitor her temperature and breathing through the night. This lent credence to the testimony Bob and Karen had made during the trial. He also said that the behavior of Bob when he was coming out of his coma, as reported by nurse Beth Harper, his loss of memory, his seemingly indifference to the news of Kathy's death, his falling asleep quickly were not at all unusual for someone who had suffered a concussion.

Before he finished his statements he asked that further testimony from Beth Harper be heard. Miss Harper reported that, knowing this hearing was coming up, she and Dr. Moreland had persuaded Karen Bailey to have a virginity test. They reported that Karen Bailey was unquestionably a virgin.

The panel conferred to discuss these new items of evidence. Their discussion was quickly over, and presented to the State Attorney. Bob was called back to hear the verdict.

The State Attorney said, "Mr. Morganton, you have the sincere apology of the state, and of our judicial system. Upon the testimony, the documents and the evidence we have received today, we are convinced that you are innocent of the crime for which you were convicted. We are presenting this evidence to the court where you were tried with the strongest possible recommendation from this office that your conviction be reversed."

Bob said, "Thank you sir. Does this mean I will be pardoned?"

"No, not pardoned," the State Attorney replied. "Pardon implies that you were once guilty. If the court, upon the examination of this new evidence accepts our recommendation, you will be found not guilty, and everything that has been recorded against you will be completely expunged. Please believe that the state is extremely sorry for your incarceration. We regret you have lost three and a half years of your life, and wish you the very best for the years ahead. You do understand that this is not final until the verdict has been reversed in the court where you were tried. However, in light of the evidence now available, and with our recommendation, I see no possibility that your guilty verdict will stand; you will be completely exonerated."

Bob replied, "Thank you sir, but I don't believe I have lost three years of life. The God I serve is amazing, and made those three years productive and useful in accomplishing His will."

The State Attorney looked at Bob with astonishment. Bob turned to Orville Nelson, thanked him, started to shake his hand, but then embraced him. A friendship had begun that was going to last a lifetime.

Orville Nelson also was by Bob's side when he appeared before the court which had originally tried his case.

As was expected by the State Attorney's office, Bob's guilty verdict was reversed, and he was declared a free man.

Orville Nelson drove Bob back to Conner's Crossing. Bob found a motel to stay in for a few days. He stopped by Barton's Cafe, and was warmly greeted by most of the customers, although a few seemed a bit less excited by his appearance back in town. As he approached one of the tables where two couples were seated he could not help but notice that they quickly ended their conversation, and awkwardly changed the subject. However, Bonnie Barton came to him, gave him a hug and said, "Bob, if you're back in town for any time you're going to need a place to live. Have you found anything yet?" Bob answered, "No, I have reserved a motel for a week, but after that I don't know where I'm going to stay."

Bonnie said "Bob, I have an apartment above my garage. It has been vacant for years now, but if you need a place, I would be happy to clean it up and have you use it. I don't want to pry, but I can't imagine you have much money, just coming out of jail. While you're looking for work, I could defer your first couple of months rent payments."

Bob said "Bonnie you're an angel. This would really help me right now." He did not tell her that he had almost no money, and that he had been deeply concerned about how he would afford a place to live. He did thank God for once again supplying his needs at just the right time.

Roger Jones, who was still chairman of the elders of the Conner's Crossing church, told Bob that he had a second car they were hardly ever using. It has been Roger's wife's car, but her health had deteriorated, and she seldom drove the car. He told Bob he was welcome to use it for a time while he was getting re-established in town. This again met a real need, and Bob told him he would gladly repay him for the use of it as soon as he was able to secure a source of income.

When Sunday came, Bob drove back to the prison, and asked if he could attend chapel one more time. He was warmly accepted, and given opportunity to speak to the men. He told them to keep up their hopes, to realize that God is a God of mercy and forgiveness, and told them that if they, even as prisoners, would seek His will, God could make their lives useful and full. He once again returned to his theme that God is able to work all things together for the good of those who have come to sincerely love Him, and pointed to his own experience as an illustration of that. Before he left there were warm handshakes and "thanks" from the men. More than a few tears were shed. From Chaplain Grey, guard Norman Wilson and inmate Glen Markle he received affectionate embraces.

Although Bonnie Barton's apartment provided adequate housing, getting re-established in the community was difficult. On the streets many greeted him warmly, but many obviously avoided him. While most folk believed he was innocent and unjustly imprisoned for a time, others evidently had their doubts of his innocence.

Bob secured a position as a substitute teacher in the local high school. However, he had only been there a couple of weeks when the county superintendent called Bob into his office. He said "Mr. Morganton, I agreed to hire you with a firm conviction of your innocence. However there are those in the community who still suspect you were guilty, and I have had numerous complaints from parents of our students who believe you should not be in our classrooms. Some of them have told their children that if you are there, they should not go into your classroom. Some have even said to their children that if they see you on campus, they are to come home and not attend school. I know it is unfair to you, but I'm afraid I'm going to have to let you go.

Bob told the superintendent that he fully understood, and thanked him for the opportunity he had given him. Nevertheless, deep inside, this hurt greatly and Bob began to wonder if others in town would hire him, or if he would be able to secure employment in this community he had come to love.

Another elder of the Conner's Crossing church came to the rescue. Jerry Johnson who had been selected to serve as an elder while Bob had been preaching there, having learned that Bob was unemployed, found him and said, "Bob, in my real estate business I not only sell property, but I manage some rental properties. These are constantly in need of cleaning and repair. I need someone I can trust to take care of this part of the business, and if you are willing to do such work, I would love to hire you. I'll even give you a day off a week so we can play golf together again, if you'll promise to let me win."

Again, Bob saw this as a godsend, and quickly took Jerry up on the offer. He found the work enjoyable, and found that Jerry was a fair and generous employer. Although his was not a high salary job, Jerry did pay Bob more than he had expected, and again Bob had re-enforced in his mind that which had always been a sustaining conviction of his - the conviction that God is at work in this world and does work things together for the good of those who love Him.

Another rich blessing was about to fall into Bob's lap. He had given little thought to the life insurance policy that he had purchased on Kathy's life. When he was convicted, the settlement on this policy had been canceled. However one day a representative of the insurance company came to Conner's Crossing, found Bob, and told him, "Mr. Morganton you are the holder of a $300,000. policy on the life of your deceased wife. This payment was withheld because of your conviction of murdering her. However, since you have now been completely exonerated of that crime, our company owes you $300,000. If you will just fill out a few papers, a check in that amount will be sent to you." While Bob had given fleeting thought to this policy, and had phoned the company one time to enquire about it, he was given such a nebulous answer that he had not pursued the matter. He was soon to learn that it was Orville Nelson who had followed up with the insurance company to secure the payment.

Being relieved of the financial stress he had been enduring, Bob began to make some plans. First he purchased a late model used car, and gave Roger Jones a substantial amount for the time he had used his car. Roger was reluctant to take anything for loaning his car, but at Bob's insistence did accept it, saying he would give the money to the mission program of the church. Then Bob began shopping for a home, and Jerry Johnson was of immense help here. With his help Bob found a very comfortable, attractive three bedroom, bath and a half house for $180,000. He purchased it with cash, and still had some money left from the insurance settlement. Bob had never had any retirement program, so he now purchased an annuity with the remainder of the money. He felt now he could live comfortably, but not extravagantly, and settled down in the quiet community of Conner's Crossing.

A BRIGHTER DAY BREAKS

Bob's life had now become quite comfortable, but lonely. However another blessing was about to come his way. When Daniel Melton had become the preacher at Conner's Crossing, Karen, thinking that having a member of a previous preacher's family in the congregation might not be helpful to the new preacher, had begun to attend the church in Hillsborough, where Denver Newton, who had been a good friend for years, was preaching. She soon became active, leading one of the children's ministries and singing as a part of the worship praise team.

One day Denver Newton phoned Bob. He said, "Bob, your sister-in-law has been working with us about three years now, and she had been a blessing to our congregation. Still, there are a couple of other areas in which we could use some help. I hear you have learned to play guitar now, and I wonder if you would join our praise team here at Hillsborough? We also have several ministries working here, but I would like to see them coordinated a bit better. What we really could use is a family life minister who could bring our various ministries together in a way that would benefit the whole family. We have several age groups which are active, but I would like to see them working together more closely, to have some projects where families work together and share worship experiences as a family more than we do. Would you be willing to do this? This is not a full time position, but if you could come and work with us on weekends, I am convinced it would really bless our congregation."

Bob was extremely hesitant. He reminded Denver that he had been in prison for over three years and told him that some of the people in Conner's Crossing were still suspicious of him. Denver replied, "I know that Bob, but I also am convinced that you are innocent. Our leadership here feels the same way. We have not contacted you without doing extensive research. We have studied the reports of the panel that examined the evidence against you, we have been in touch with the prison personnel and the prison chaplain and have learned of the excellent work you did with the penitentiary chapel. We have three former inmates in our congregation, and our leadership is convinced you would be the ideal person to fill the needs of our church family. Your working with us would be an encouragement to these inmates during their time of rehabilitation and reorientation into society."

Bob agreed to give the possibility prayerful consideration. He told Denver he would come to Hillsborough to worship the next Sunday, and would talk with him about the matter. Bob rode with Karen that Sunday as she traveled to Hillsborough. He and Denver had a long talk in the afternoon. Bob agreed to come and work with Denver in the Hillsborough ministry.

After just two Sundays, Denver Newton had another proposal for Bob. He said, "Bob, we talked about you being here with us for the weekends. If you could come here on Friday evening we would be glad to have you stay in our home Friday and Saturday nights, or even Sunday night if you wanted to. I know you and Karen have been driving here together, and there is a family in the church who have two teen-age daughters. They all love Karen, and would be delighted if she would stay with them over the weekends."

Bob told Denver he would give him an answer the following Sunday.

Driving home that Sunday evening Bob talked the matter over with Karen. They agreed they would think about it for a week, and come to a decision by the following Sunday. As they reached Bob's house, they joined hands and prayed together about the matter. As they clasped hands, Bob again felt that surge of pleasure he had known when Karen had been near him on much earlier occasions. Even after they had finished their prayer, their hands remained clasped for several moments.

Bob said he would drive the following Sunday, and as Karen got in his car to begin the trip, Bob grasped her hand, and said "Let's pray together about this decision we've got to make, and ask God to bless our trip and our ministry with the Hillsborough church." As they did, Bob again felt the deep pleasure of Karen's hand clasped in his. After the prayer Karen said, "I have been considering Denver's proposal all week, and I find it rather exciting. I would really like to do it." Bob answered, "I was hoping that's what you would say. It will open a new field of ministry for me, and I must confess, I have really enjoyed traveling and working with you in this weekend ministry. We will alternate the weeks we drive, and we'll pray the Lord will use us in a fruitful way in this new door he has opened for us."

All week long Bob found himself looking forward to his weekend ministry, and especially to the drive to and from Hillsborough with Karen. Each Sunday evening as they arrived back in Conner's Crossing Bob would say, "We make a pretty good team, don't we Karen," and Karen would answer "I really feel we do."

Bob continued his work in maintaining rental apartments for Jerry Johnson. He also continued to take Buddy Barton, who was now getting too big to be called "Little Buddy, to school in the morning and then have breakfast at Barton's Cafe.

At Daniel Melton's invitation, often Bob would drop in on the elder's breakfast that was still being held on a Tuesday morning every other month in Barton's Cafe. He usually waited until the meeting was nearly over, and would just have a cup of coffee with them during the casual part of their discussions. He enjoyed the fellowship with the four elders of the church, and with their preacher. They also seemed to appreciate his participation, and often asked him about his weekend ministry in Hillsborough.

Bob felt himself growing in his appreciation and affection for Bonnie Barton for the kindness she continued to show him. She had become one of his closest friends. One day he said to her, "Bonnie, I'm concerned about you. You work too hard, and have a tired look most of the time. It amazes me that you maintain your cheery, upbeat attitude all the time when I know you must be bone tired. Your business has grown nicely, you now have additional income from the apartment you continued to rent after I moved out, and I believe you could afford to close the cafe' on Sundays. God doesn't intend for anyone to work seven days a week without rest. You really need to have a time of worship and rest in your life. Why don't you close the cafe' on Sundays, begin attending worship regularly, and give yourself a day of rest and renewal?"

Bonnie replied, "I know I should, but I have so many customers who come in for breakfast early Sunday morning, and then go to church. I also have some who come in after church for lunch. I don't believe it would be fair to them if I were to close Sundays."

Bob said "I understand your concern for them. But Bonnie, you can't keep this up forever. I don't believe you're being fair to yourself if you don't slow down some. Your own health is involved. Please consider what I say."

Bonnie looked apprehensive, and said, "I've been doing this for ten years now, and really don't know if I can change. I really feel that even though I have not been attending church, I have been providing a ministry for those who do."

Bob replied, "Bonnie, what you say is an indication of the kind of person you are. I appreciate that deeply. I believe you must be a praying person, and I only ask that you consider what I say, and give the matter some prayerful thought."

When the preacher and elders met at Barton's Cafe' the second Tuesday of the month, they noticed a sign in the window: BEGINNING THE FIRST OF NEXT MONTH, THIS CAFE WILL BE CLOSED ON SUNDAYS.

Some of her customers grumbled when they heard that news. Others said, "Bonnie, I know you have been overworked. I believe you have made a wise choice."

The difference in Bonnie was surprisingly rapid. The sparkle in her eyes, long obscured by the dark circles that had often surrounded them, was more brilliant as those dark circles faded. There was a spring in her step. Her voice, always cheerful and uplifting, was even more inviting and pleasant. In spite of the loss of one day of business, her clientele grew. She was able to hire two more employees, and have someone she trusted who would oversee the clean up and closing after the evening meal hour. This made it possible for Bonnie to go home by eight o'clock each evening.

One Tuesday morning, as the church leaders and Bob were concluding their time together at the cafe, Bonnie came up behind Bob's chair. She placed her hands on his shoulders, gave him a kiss on the side of his face, and said, "Bob, thank you for your suggestion to close one day a week, spend time in worship and get some rest on Sundays. I feel ten years younger."

Usually when he was leaving the cafe' after breakfast, and sometimes after the meeting there with the leaders of the church, Bob would grasp the point of Bonnie's chin between his thumb and forefinger and give her a quick kiss on her forehead. Roger Jones, still chairman of the elders, noticed this. He also noticed that Bonnie would at times be seen trying to straighten her body and lift her head as though she were trying to get her lips, rather than her forehead, on a level with Bob's lips. This concerned him to the point that one day after they had stepped out of the cafe' Roger said, "Bob, I don't want to meddle in your private life, but there is something that really concerns me. I wonder what your relationship with Bonnie really is. I notice the friendly little kiss you place on her forehead at times. I don't know if that means much to you, but I think it means more to Bonnie than you may want it to. If you are seriously interested in her and see a deepening of your relationship, that would be fine. She is an outstanding woman, attractive, intelligent and certainly industrious. I don't know if you realize it, but she has deep feelings for you. Her employees have told me that you are all she thinks of or talks about. They say at work she is always saying, 'Bob said this,' or 'Bob did this.' And her son, Buddy, idolizes you. You are his hero. If you are thinking of a future together with her, I know of no one who would make you a better wife or of no one who would make a better husband for her and a better father for Buddy than you would. If that is in your future, I want you to know you would have my unreserved blessing. However, if these are not your intentions, I think you need to let Bonnie know that. I'm sure a future with you is prominent in her thoughts and hopes."

Roger's statement plunged Bob into deep thought which he could not get out of his mind. He did have a deep affection for Bonnie, and for Buddy as well. For days the thought of marrying Bonnie and being the kind of husband she needed and the kind of father that Buddy wanted dominated his waking hours. Bonnie was three years older than Bob, but the recent rejuvenation she had experienced gave her a younger look and vigor. Bob had to admit his own loneliness. He believed that marrying Bonnie would be completely within God's will.

But there was the growing attraction he had to Karen, who was six years younger than Bob. The excitement he felt when they were together could not be denied. He prayed for weeks seeking direction from God.

The matter came to a head one evening as he and Karen returned from their trip to Hillsborough. When he said, "Karen, we do make a good team, don't we?" instead of her usual reply, "Yes, I really believe we do," she replied with "Yes, we do, but Bob, is that all it's ever going to be?"

"What do you mean?" Bob asked.

Karen said, "Bob, I've got to make up my mind about some things. As you know, after Kathy died and you were sent to prison I rented two bedrooms in my house. One of them was to one of the hospital administrators and the other to Dr. Alan Kingsley, Dr. Kingsley came to us as a young intern, but has now completed his internship and is on staff as a doctor at the medical center. We often have lunch together in the cafeteria, and he has become a close friend. Alan has become a fine doctor and has a promising future. Recently he has made it clear to me that he wants to be more than just a tenant in my house, a fellow worker in the hospital and a good friend. As he worded it, he would like to take our relationship 'to the next level.'

Bob, I don't know if I should encourage him or not." "Why shouldn't you?" Bob asked as he felt a tightening in his stomach.

Karen's voice shook, and her chin began to tremble as she responded. "Bob, you've said time and again we make a good team. I can't deny I have wondered repeatedly if our relationship would go beyond that. I feel a closeness to you like nothing I have felt since Kathy and Dad died. You are my brother-in-law, but I feel as close to you as I did to my flesh and blood sister and as I now do to my brothers. And yet I am not content with just a brother - sister relationship with you. I have felt an attraction that I believe you have felt also." Tears were now starting down Karen's cheeks. "I have detected it when you have continued holding my hand after we have finished our praying together. Perhaps it's been wishful thinking, but I have thought I have detected it several times as we have worked together. Honestly, I must admit I could not give my heart completely to Dr. Kingsley in my present state of mind. God has first place in my heart, but Bob, you have a huge part of it too."

Bob struggled to find his voice. Then he said, "Karen, you have been right in detecting my attraction for you. It's been there for a long time, and it's growing stronger and stronger. I have tried to deny it because I know if we become romantically involved there will be those who will believe I really did have a deliberate part in Kathy's death. There are still those who believe I did, or at least when around me it seems to me they believe I did. I am concerned about what our becoming more deeply involved would do to our Christian witness. In spite of the time I did as a prisoner, God has now given us both an opportunity to serve Him again, and should you and I let it be seen that we are serious about each other I'm afraid the effectiveness of our witness would be hampered. Paul writes about the need to take extreme care to avoid placing a stumbling block in the way of a brother. He wrote that even though all meats had been made clean by our Lord, that if eating meat would cause a brother to stumble he would refrain from eating meat. He even said in Romans 14:16 'do not let what you considered good to be spoken of as evil.' Karen, our witness before people is vital; the salvation of some even depend on it. I think of that all the time, and because of what others may think I have hidden my affection for you from the public, from you, and I've even tried to deny it to myself."

Karen responded, "Bob, I don't know scripture as well as you do, but I do know that Paul said he would not allow himself to be brought under the judgment of man, but was totally subject to the judgment of God."

"You're thinking of the 4th chapter of I Corinthians," Bob interjected. Karen went on "I knew he had said that, and I also remember that the apostles once said 'we must obey God rather than man.' Bob, I have always greatly admired your deep conviction, and I still do, but I believe you're letting an over sensitive conscience interfere with your own happiness, and perhaps not seeing what God's will really is in this matter."

Bob sat silently for what seemed a long time. Then he took both of Karen's hands in his hands and said, "Karen, we really need to seek God's will in this matter. Let's both pray about it tonight."

And pray they did. Karen through sobs, and Bob in spite of repeated times he paused to hold back his own sobs . When they had finished their prayers they continued to hold hands for a time. Their faces came closer and closer together until Bob said, "Well, we've got to do some serious thinking and praying. Both of us have to be at work in the morning, so we'd better say goodnight, and leave our future in the hands of God." Both of them had trouble falling asleep that night.

In the coming days the comments of Roger Jones about Bonnie Barton and his own conversation with Karen were on Bob's mind constantly. He was thankful that his work through the week was now pretty much manual labor, because he would have had trouble keeping his mind on anything that required deep concentration or close attention. He had a strange mix of emotions as he thought of his trip to Hillsborough on Friday evening. He had the usual excitement and pleasant anticipation of being with Karen, but an unusual and uneasy anxiety about what their conversation might be, and where it might take them.

And the trip was rather strained. Their conversation was about things related to the work with the Hillsborough church, and they seemed to rehash things that had already been worked out. Both of them knew that below the surface were much deeper thoughts that still needed to be resolved. For two folks as open and close to each other as they had been, it was a strange experience for both of them. When they clasped hands for the prayer they always shared together, both as they were leaving on Friday and when they returned on Sunday night, Bob was aware that Karen's hands were trembling. When they had concluded their prayer Sunday evening Bob sat in silence with his head still bowed for a time, grasping Karen's hands so tightly that it almost hurt her. Then he lifted his head, drew Karen's hands to him, and kissed her hands before he said goodnight.

Monday Bob decided he must have that talk with Bonnie. He had been searching his heart, and knew what he had to say. He did have a love for Bonnie born out of his admiration for her and the affection that had grown between them when she had stepped in to provide housing and help at a time when he greatly needed it. That affection, appreciation and admiration had grown while he had lived in her apartment and eaten at the cafe' almost every morning during the months school was in session. He also had a deep affection for Buddy. He realized he could have a good life with her and provide the father figure that Buddy so desperately needed in the home.

Tuesday night Bob went to the cafe' at 8:00 o'clock, the time Bonnie usually went home. He said he wanted to talk with her. Bonnie's heart leaped within from a combination of eager anticipation and fear. Bonnie told the two who usually did the clean up and closing after the evening customers left that they could go home, and that she would take care of closing up. Bob helped her with that, and after Bonnie had locked the door and turned off all but the night lights, they sat down at a table together.

Bob began: "Bonnie, perhaps what I'm about to say is unnecessary and I may look like a fool for saying it, but I really don't want to leave any false impressions. Both you and Buddy have become very precious to me, and I know I will carry you both in my heart all my life."

"But...." Bonnie said.

Realizing now that Bonnie was anticipating what he was about to say, Bob went on. "I care a lot for you, and I'm sure you know that. However, I hope the affection I have shown for you hasn't left impressions that I need to correct. Maybe our relationship doesn't mean enough to you for me to be concerned, but I must admit I have been concerned enough that I have given considerable thought to what our future together may be. I have even thought about the possibility of our marrying, and have wondered if that thought has ever entered your mind. Perhaps it never has, and if it hasn't I am making a first class fool of myself."

Bonnie interrupted: "Bob, you are no fool. That has been my hope for some months now." Bob could tell Bonnie was steeling herself to keep her composure as she continued on. "However, from what you are saying I think you are trying to tell me that you do not anticipate us have a deeper relationship or sharing our lives in the future."

Bob went on: "Bonnie, I will always have a deep love for you and Buddy. I sincerely hope that never changes. I want us to be close friends as long as we live, but to say I feel we should marry would be unfair to you. There is something that keeps me from making that kind of a commitment."

With tears now streaming down her cheeks, Bonnie said, "It's Karen, isn't it?"

Bob was astonished at Bonnie's perception. "How did you know?" he asked.

Bonnie said, "Bob, I know you better than you think. I also know Karen very well. I've seen the way she looks at you. I've seen the way you treat her. I'm sure Karen is in love with you, and I think you are in love with her. I love both of you, and I want you both to have all the happiness in the world. It breaks my heart to say so, but if you and I aren't meant to be, I wish you and Karen the very best."

As they rose to leave the table, Bob again took Bonnie's chin between his forefinger and thumb and placed a kiss, on her forehead. This time not a quick one, but a lingering one. Then they fell into a long embrace.

That night Bob rehearsed all the scripture in his mind over and over again before he fell asleep. Bonnie Barton cried herself to sleep.

The Friday evening drive to Hillsborough with Karen was a strained one; little conversation and periods of awkward silence. Yet each knew what was on the other's mind. Through Saturday and Sunday, with each of them busy in their ministries with the church, things went well. As they were returning on Sunday night Bob and Karen knew that the conversation they had two weeks earlier had be continued. After driving just a few minutes in silence, they both began to speak at once. As Bob was saying, "Karen, we need to talk more about our future," Karen was saying, "Bob, I have been uncomfortable since our conversation two weeks ago." They broke into laughter, and the tension eased. Then Bob said, "O.K. Karen, you tell me what is on your mind first." She began: "Bob, I have given much thought to what you said two weeks ago, and I still believe that you should not let the concern you have about what other people might think rob us of happiness we can have together. But something else has occurred to me; are you becoming seriously interested in me because you look at me, whether you realize it or not, as a substitute for my sister? I know you are lonely, and I also know how much you loved Kathy. The tenderness and the care you showed for her during those last years when Kathy was not well, even when, let's face it, it was obvious she must have become very hard to live with, was a testimony of your deep and pure love for her. I must confess it was watching you during that time that my admiration for you began to really grow. It is also that loving care that makes anyone who knows you at all sure that you could have had no intentions to harm her. But Bob, my sister was a beautiful woman, and I will wonder each time you look into my eyes, or times when you might declare your love for me, will you be seeing Karen or Kathy?"

As Karen had been talking, Bob pulled the car to a sparsely occupied parking lot at the side of the road. He wanted to respond undistracted by attention to his driving. He turned to look fully into Karen's face, "Oh, my darling" (the term came surprisingly naturally and easily from his lips) "my love for you; there, I've said it, I love you, my love for you is genuine and is related to none other than Karen Bailey. You are right, I did love Kathy right up to the end. But I love you as Karen; not because you are my deceased wife's sister but because you are Karen, a precious and beautiful and desirable woman. You are not a substitute for anyone! You are the one with whom I want to share my heart and the rest of my life."

The planning for the wedding was complicated, not because of difficulty choosing those who would participate in it, but of deciding whom they could not include. Karen and Bob both had many friends in Conner's Crossing and in Hillsborough. It was decided that Denver Newton, their good preacher friend with whom they had worked in ministry at Hillsborough, would perform the ceremony. Roger Jones, chairman of the elders would be Bob's Best Man. Lester and Alvin Bailey, Karen's brothers. Jerry Johnson and Clarence White, also elders at the Conner's Crossing church would be groomsmen. Orville Nelson, the editor, and John Black, the other elder at Conner's Crossing church would be ushers. Dr. Marvin Moreland would give the bride away.

Although she sobbed and fought tears all through the ceremony, Bonnie Barton was Karen's Matron of Honor. Beth Harper and three other of Karen's fellow employees were bridesmaids. The wedding was beautiful, a deeply spiritual affair, but also a joyous celebration.

After the wedding, Karen moved into the house Bob had purchased, and the large house in which Karen had grown up became a rental property, and was occupied by 5 of the medical center personnel. However, within four years it became obvious that the house Bob had purchased was getting too small for Bob and Karen's growing family.

Ruth was the first child to be born to Bob and Karen fifteen months after their wedding. Two years later Phillip was born. Eight months after Phillip's birth Karen was pregnant again, the happy couple decided that with the family growing they needed to consider a larger house, so Bob and Karen sold the house where they were living, and moved back into the place where Karen had grown up, and where Bob and Kathy had lived during the years of his ministry with the Conner's Crossing congregation.

Bob still worked with Jerry Johnson's real estate company, and Karen kept her job with the Medical Center. They also continued their week-end ministry with the Hillsborough church. Their days and hours were filled with activity. Although Karen had taken considerable time off from the Medical Center for child birth and about a year after those births to take care of the babies, the Medical Center had kept her job open for her, and each time she had gone back to work. Fortunately, the Conner's Crossing church had developed an excellent child care program, and Ruth, Phillip and Steven, the third child, were taken there when Karen went back to work. Both Bob and Karen loved being parents, and as soon as her work hours, which had now been changed to an 8:00 to 4:00 o'clock schedule were up at the Medical Center, Karen would go immediately to the church to pick up the children. There were some days, when Bob did not have obligations with Jerry Johnson's rental business that he would pick up the children for the afternoon. So while they were always busy, they still gave priority to what Bob and Karen both considered their primary God-given responsibility, giving loving care and guidance to their children.

With the sale of the home Bob had purchased, he and Karen had a long discussion. The cost of child care was significant, but God had provided their needs adequately, and they had no mortgages to pay. Although they had little in discretionary funds, they were meeting all their obligations. Bob said to Karen, "Honey we have been blessed, and God is continuing to bless us. You are building a retirement fund from the Medical Center, and I have an annuity that will still have some left to pay a small amount at my retirement. I believe that God would have us consider the fact that we need more for our senior years. My Alma Mater, Clovernook Seminary, is in a capital funds campaign to make some needed expansion of the campus. They are offering an opportunity to purchase annuities which would help them in their present need, and which we could have available for our retirement years. It would mean we would have to live rather frugally for the next few years, but I believe it would be a good stewardship investment for two reasons. It would help the seminary in its present situation, and would provide that retirement investment we need to make. I honestly believe it would be a win-win situation."

After a few days of prayer, the entire amount they had received from the sale of the home was given to Clovernook Seminary as a gift annuity.

These were extremely busy, but gloriously happy days for the Bob Morganton family. Karen joined Bob in their daily thanksgiving to God for working all things out for their good. They were even more excited when they learned that a fourth child was on its way to join the family.

Then one day the call came. It was surprising and exciting, but challenged Bob to make one of the most difficult decisions of his life. It was from the Rockview church where Bob had led a seminar and preached just before Kathy's death. Their preacher, Glen Coleman was on the line. He said, "Brother Morganton, I'm here with the elders of our congregation. We have the phone on speaker at the church office, and we can all hear what you are saying. I don't suppose you have heard, but I am retiring here at Rockview, and for the past several months we have had a pulpit committee meeting and searching for my replacement. The elders have been working with them, and it is now their unanimous consensus that we want to ask you to consider the ministry here. I know you well enough to realize that your first response is that you want to pray about the matter, but please give it some serious, thoughtful prayer. If you are willing to pursue the matter, we would like you to come and meet with us for further interviews. After those interviews, if we continue to feel as we do now, we would present your name to the congregation and have you preach again as they consider extending the call for you to become our preacher here."

Bob's whole body was shaking. He could not answer, and brother Coleman said, "Bob, are you still there?"

"Yes, I'm here" Bob answered when he had regained some composure. "I'm shocked and astounded that you should call. You realize don't you, that I was a suspect in my wife's death, and have done over three years of prison time? For several years now I have been out of the preaching ministry."

"We know that Bob," Glen responded. "But we also know other things about you. Our search committee has been thorough. We followed your trial, and the news reports that Orville Nelson made of it and of your ministry even while in prison. We have conferred with Chaplain Grey and with the prison personnel. We have talked with brother Newton and some of the leadership at the Hillsborough church. Every one of them is totally convinced of your innocence of the charges against you, and gave glowing recommendations of you."

Bob was still wrestling with his surprise at their call. "Brother Coleman," he said, "I am not only surprised, but actually shocked, at your invitation. I felt I had done a miserable job on the sermon I preached on the Sunday morning I was with you. I never expected to hear from you again."

"You thought you did a miserable job?" brother Coleman said with almost as much surprise in his voice as there had been in Bob's. "I want you to know that your sermon on 'This is the Victory that

Overcomes the World, even our Faith' so impressed our congregation that we took it as a theme for our programming here. Our slogan for the past several years has been 'Faith That Overcomes.' The Lord has blessed us with consistent growth and we now regularly have over 1200 in attendance. We believe you are the man to lead us in continued, and even greater, growth."

Glen Coleman was right. Bob did ask for time to give prayerful consideration to this opportunity. With Karen he began a concerted few days of prayer. They asked God to make His will clear to them. They were happy in the part time ministry in which they were presently involved together. They had precious friends in both Conner's Crossing and Hillsborough. Karen loved her work at the Medical Center, and Bob enjoyed his work with and his close friendship with Jerry Johnson. There were many close attachments and associations that would be severed by such a move. It would not be easy to leave a community they had both come to love.

But yet the call of God seemed clear in the fact that the Rockview church had approached them when Bob and Karen had made no efforts on their own to find a new ministry. Bob had always believed that if God had a place He wanted him to serve, that call would come from God without Bob's pursuing his own agenda. So far in his life this had always been the case. When this opportunity and challenge had been placed before him, Bob could not dismiss the thought that it must be the leading of the Lord.

The following week Bob agreed to meet with the elders and the pulpit committee of the Rockview church. Their meeting was cordial and positive. It was agreed that Bob would be recommended to the congregation, and he would come and preach prior to a congregational vote to extend the call to him. Ninety six percent of the voting membership were in favor of extending the call for Bob to come and be their preacher.

Bob and Karen, with Ruth, Phillip, Steven and their newborn daughter Esther, began making plans for their move. They were to move to Rockview three months before the time Bob was expected to begin his preaching responsibilities. During that time he would attend services there, meet with the elders, with the deacons and with the staff members and various committees during their meetings. This allowed him to get a feel for what had been going on with the congregation. He was made very welcome at these meetings, and was invited to share his visions for the future of the congregation. The transition was amicable and smooth, and Bob and his family entered their new ministry at Rockview with joyous anticipation.

CONVICTION RECONFIRMED

The Rockview church provided a generous salary plus an expense account and a housing allowance. With their move to Rockview, Karen and Bob decided to sell the large house in which Karen had lived most of her life. Realizing that their financial needs were well provided, they discussed what to do with the money they received from the sale. Karen remarked that Dr. Moreland had been raising funds to build a small hospital for the mission enterprise where he had volunteered his time. After prayer, they decided to give the entire amount of the sale price to Dr. Moreland for the hospital in Haiti. When they had made the gift, they agreed that it was one of the most gratifying and satisfying things they had ever done. Bob remarked "Jesus was exactly right when He said, 'It is more blessed to give than it is to receive' wasn't he?" Smiling broadly, Karen answered, "He certainly was.'"

Bob's heart was overflowing with gratitude. In spite of the loss of his wife, his unjust imprisonment and the deep sorrows that had often invaded his life, Bob never lost his confidence in the providence of God; and his conviction that for those who love God all things do work together for good. He had seen the hand of God at work through all his trials. However, now he began to experience the goodness of God to a degree beyond anything he had known before.

CONVICTION RECONFIRMED

He and Karen were deliriously happy as husband and wife. His long held, fervent desire to be a father had now found fulfillment in the birth of two sons and two daughters. Bob realized that promise he had so long anticipated from Psalm 127:3,4 "Behold, children are a heritage from the Lord, the fruit of the womb is His reward. Like arrows in the hand of a warrior, so are the children of one's youth. Happy is the man who has his quiver full of them." While Bob was now in his forties, and his delight in fatherhood had been long delayed, he still constantly rejoiced in the faithfulness of God in bringing to fruition his fervent and life-long desires. He had a beautiful family and a challenging ministry. He prayed that the Lord would count him worthy of such blessings, and would bless his ministry with fruit that would glorify God.

And God was answering that prayer in a magnificent and undeniable way. Attendance was growing rapidly and steadily. A ministry to the homeless in the community was established. The mission support of the congregation increased markedly. The congregation was known for its compassionate outreach beyond the walls of its building. The city and the surrounding area were feeling the impact of the dynamic ministry of the Rockview church. A new congregation twelve miles away in a community where several of the members of the congregation lived was planted. Even though this took a significant number of the regular attendees at Rockview away, their growth still continued, and the need for larger facilities was becoming evident.

A campaign was begun to raise funds for a new building. Bob was again surprised, nearly overwhelmed in fact, by the response and sacrifice of the congregation. Within three years the needed finances were provided, and a new worship center was constructed. The former building was converted into a family life center. Within four years from the time they began the construction of their new facility the congregation was having an attendance of over 1500 per Sunday. There was hardly ever a week when new members were not added to the congregation.

When they had moved to Rockview, Bob and Karen had purchased a very large, very old house. The house had four bedrooms and two and a half baths. The living room was large and it had an eat-in kitchen plus a dining room and a den. However, while it was large and commodious, it was old and much in need of repair. It had a lot of charm, and seemed to speak of gracious living in days gone by. It's age and need of repair had made the price reasonable for such a large home. Bob realized that he could put the skills and experience he had gained while working for Jerry Johnson's real estate company to good use.

Bob had always preferred to take Thursday as his day off. He had found Saturday to be cluttered with last minute preparations that had to be made for the Sunday services. Also, he needed time on Saturday to put the final touches on his Sunday sermons. He told the leadership of the church that he would be using most Thursdays to work on his house. The leadership of the church was supportive of this, and some of the retired men in the congregation began showing up quite regularly to give him help. He was surprised and gratified at this, and so with this help and some evening hours Bob managed to use for house repair, the refurbishing of the house moved much more quickly than Bob had anticipated. Soon Bob, Karen, Ruth, Phillip, Steven and Esther were enjoying a fine, larger and comfortable home. Once again Bob was aware of the amazing grace of God flowing to His servants.

While the house was being refurbished Bob spent three Thursdays of most months working on the house. However, he still kept one

Thursday a month for golf with his old buddies from Conner's Crossing. Sometimes he drove to Conner's Crossing County Club, but some months the men drove over to Rockview, and other times they met at a course about half way between the two. Bob's deceased father-in-law had once been a part of their foursome, but now William Alvers, one of the elders of the Rockview church, joined them for their golfing. William enjoyed the fellowship with these men, and a warm contact between the leaders of the Rockview and Conner's Crossing congregations developed. However, due to the declining health of his wife, Roger Jones often missed these golfing get-togethers, and on those occasions Orville Nelson, the editor of the <u>Conner's Crossing Crier</u> filled out the foursome.

In a few months Roger Jones' participation with the golfing foursome stopped entirely as his wife's health continued to deteriorate. Then one Thursday as they met for their round of golf Jerry Johnson said, "Bob, we've got some sad news this morning. Roger's wife, Sue, died yesterday. Her memorial service is planned for Saturday afternoon at the Conner' Crossing church."

As soon as Bob got home from his round of golf, he and Karen began immediately to make their plans to go as a family to Conner's Crossing for the funeral. The service was planned as a celebration for Sue's life. It was a bitter sweet affair. Reunion with the family of the Conner's Crossing church was a blessing to Bob and his family. The shedding of tears at the parting of one who had been a precious and valuable servant of the Lord all her life was mixed with fond memories expressed by dozen's of people whose lives had been touched and blessed by Sue. Bob was thankful for his opportunity to be with Roger Jones and to share this time of sorrow with one who had been such an encouragement and support to him during his ministry. Once again they wept together at the loss of one whom

CONVICTION RECONFIRMED

they both loved and at the same time rejoiced at the glories they knew that Sue was now enjoying with her Lord.

Roger began to meet again with his golfing buddies. On some of the monthly Thursday golf outings both Roger and Orville Nelson would come with the men from Conner's Crossing. On those occasions two of the men from the Rockview church would play with them, and rather than a foursome they would play as two threesomes. The lunch and fellowship the six shared together after eighteen holes was a warm and relaxing time. All month long these men, united in their shared love of the Lord, looked forward to these Thursdays.

Yet for the next few of their monthly golf get-to-gathers it was obvious that Roger was not his usual positive self. His enthusiasm for the game seemed to have waned. During their lively, jovial conversations at lunch after they had finished their round of golf Roger was almost silent. Formerly he laughed robustly at Jerry Johnson's jokes and antics, but now he just chuckled at them. Bob attributed this change in behavior to the sadness and loneliness Roger was still feeling from the loss of his wife. Bob began praying that Roger would not fall into the deep depression that had beset Kathy after the loss of their first child and then the loss of her father.

He believed his prayers were being answered when there was a noticeable change in Roger's attitude. The spring returned to his step. His smile which had almost vanished became more frequent. Once again he obviously enjoyed golf. He played with the vigor he had shown ten years earlier. His hearty laugh returned.

Fourteen months later Bob learned the reason for this late middle-aged man's return to his youthful vigor. As they were waiting to tee off one morning, Roger said, "Bob, I've some news for you, and I want to ask a favor." Bob responded, "Tell me the news, and you know I'll do anything I can for you." Roger had seemed almost giddy as he waited anxiously to share this news. He revealed the news and asked the favor in one statement: "Bob, I'd like you to be my best man."

Bob was a bit surprised, but elated. He now understood why Roger had displayed such a noticeable rejuvenation. "Why of course I will, I'd be proud to be your best man." Bob said. "Tell me, who is the lucky woman? Is it anyone I know."

"It sure is," said Roger. "Bonnie Barton and I are getting married."

Bob let out a shout, "Hallelujah! Bonnie is a wonderful woman, and you will be an ideal husband for her. This is the best news I've heard in years."

Bob could hardly wait to get home to call Bonnie to congratulate her. She responded to his congratulations by saying, "Bob, I'm so happy. You know I was in love with you, and heartbroken when you told me you were going to marry Karen. But I have now fallen deeply in love with Roger. He is about the most understanding, kindest man I have ever known. It took me a while, but now I see the hand of God in all that has happened." Bob said, "Bonnie, I'm so thankful that Roger asked me to have a part in your wedding. I'm going to pray, and I know God will bless you and Roger with a lasting and wonderful marriage and life together."

MANY ROSES, BUT A FEW THORNS

While Bob lived with the conviction that all things work together for those who love God, he was not so naive as to believe that even the best of people did not have their difficulties and troubles in life. Two of these storms came within his own family.

Bob and his family had been making a two week trip each year to work with the mission in Haiti where Dr. Moreland contributed so much of his time. On one of these trips two siblings, four year old Ramón and his sister, two year old Ramona caught their eyes and stole their hearts. They were extremely polite and winsome children. They always said "please" and "thank you," "Sir" and "Maam". Yet they were shy and withdrawn, and seemed to be afraid of nearly everyone. They smiled weakly, but almost never laughed.

Their mother visited frequently, and the children always were delighted to see her. Sometimes the father and mother visited together, but on those occasions Ramón and Ramona would sit on their mother's lap, but obviously avoided their father. As Bob and Karen looked into the matter they found the situation was even more severe than they had suspected. As they had guessed, their father had abused the children, hence their avoidance of him when they visited. He was addicted to both alcohol and drugs. His unrestrained life style had left him with HIV. The children's parents were not divorced, but they had not lived together since Ramona had been born.

Legal authorities had decreed that the father could not see the children unless his wife was with him. He seemed unconcerned about this. He did not seem at all bothered that his children avoided him when he was around. On the other hand, the affection between Ramón and Ramona and their mother was evidently warm. It was obvious she loved them deeply and they loved her.

While she had tried her very best to care for her son and daughter alone, the time came when she realized she could not provide the secure home they needed. With great reluctance she had turned them over to the care of the children's home the mission operated. She visited her children weekly, and spent several hours with them each time. Wanting what was best for them, the mother had told the administration of the children's home that, although it would break her heart, if a good home could be found for the children, she would give them up for adoption to the right kind of parents. The father had no objection to this.

During their visit, Bob and Karen had fallen in love with the children, and were very fond of their mother. One evening Bob and Karen learned that the children had been put up for adoption. They went to bed early. They lay silently side-by-side, each of them knowing what was on the other's mind. Finally Karen spoke first: "Bob, are you thinking what I'm thinking?"

"I probably am, Honey. I can't get Ramón, Ramona and their mother off my mind" said Bob.

"Neither can I," Karen said. "It's hard to know what would be best for them. The children's home here does a magnificent job, but certainly the children would be better off in a traditional family."

I believe they would too" Bob replied.

"But yet" Karen said, "separating them from their mother seems cruel. It is evident that they deeply love her, and without doubt she loves them. As a mother, I can't imagine the pain of being separated from such beautiful children."

"I know what you mean." Bob hesitated before he went on. "But, Karen, if it would be best for them, as their mother is convinced it would be, has it entered your mind that we might consider adopting Ramón and Ramona?"

"You know it has. I know that this would be a huge decision for them as well as for us. We need to pray hard about this."

"Certainly we do." Bob replied. "Many lives are involved here; Ramón's, Ramona's, their mother's, our lives and our children's lives. I don't know when we've had to face a more weighty decision."

They both lay awake for a long time that night, praying and seeking God's guidance. And the prayer continued for the several days before their return back to the United States and their ministry in Rockview. They did not mention these things to Ruth, Phillip, Steven and Esther, but they did talk with the children's home administration and with Ramón and Ramona's mother before they left. The administrators said they had worked with the adoption agencies before, and yes, the children could be adopted. The children's mother, Theresa. said, "If my children could be in a home like your's, that would be an answer to my prayers." Then she burst into uncontrolled tears.

Bob and Karen told Theresa that the matter was not yet fully settled. They still had to talk to their children. They wanted Theresa to give more thought to make sure she really wanted to give her children up for adoption. They told her that if they took the children, when they made their annual trip to Haiti they would bring Ramón and Ramona with them and they would try hard to arrange for her to come to visit them in Rockview frequently.

Ruth and Phillip were now in high school, and Steven and Esther were in middle school. One evening after supper, a few days after they returned to Rockview, Bob and Karen brought up the anticipated adoption with the children. Bob said, "We want the four of you to know that your mother and I have been considering adopting Ramón and Ramona."

The surprise and shock was evident on the faces of all four children. Bob paused for a moment and then went on. "You know Ramón and Ramona need a family, and their mother, though deeply grieved at the thought of separation from them, wants them to have prospects of a better future than they now have. If they were to come and live with us, we would have to make some changes. Ruth, I know you and Esther each have your own bedroom, but if we follow through on this adoption, you would have to move into one bedroom, or else one of you would have to take Ramona into your room."

"No way," shouted Ruth. "I'm not going to give up my privacy for anyone. Not my sister, not Ramona, or anyone."

Karen, with admirable composure said, "Ruth, please be patient and hear us out. Do you realize what a blessing you and Esther could be to this little girl's life?"

"I don't care," Ruth retorted. She crossed her arms in defiance and slumped down in her chair. Esther was also scowling with a look of belligerence.

Bob continued, "I'm sorry you girls feel this way. I would ask you to examine your attitude and realize what an opportunity this could be for you to really make a difference in other's lives. And you boys would have to make some changes too. You are sharing a room now, and we would have to find a place for Ramón. Your mother and I have the largest bedroom in the house, and we would move your double bed into our room and still have space for another single bed. Your mother and I would move into your room."

MANY ROSES, BUT A FEW THORNS

Phillip and Steven answered in almost unison. "Not cool, Dad." Phillip said, "We need our space, and you and Mom need to keep your own room."

Bob was deeply disappointed. While the whole family ordinarily stayed and cleaned up the kitchen and washed the dishes together, this evening all four of their children stomped loudly out of the room. Ruth and Esther both slammed their bedroom doors in anger.

Bob and Karen sat silently and looked at each other with dismay. Karen broke their silence by saying, "Well dear, I guess we'll have to give up the thought of adopting Ramón and Ramona. I'm a bit shocked and really disappointed at our own children tonight, but they are the children God has given us, and they are our primary responsibility. This idea hit them suddenly tonight. Perhaps after they think it over a while their attitudes will soften a bit."

Bob never "targeted" anyone with his sermons. His practice was to preach expository sermons, simply explaining and clarifying the meaning of a passage of Scripture. Usually he preached in a series, often just preaching through a book of the Bible. He believed that such preaching would meet the needs of people, would instruct and challenge them to righteous living, without him having to decide who needed to be "preached at" in any particular sermon. As he was preparing for his sermon for the coming Sunday he was in a dilemma. He was in a series on the Sermon on the Mount, and was going to preach on Matthew 7:12, "So in everything, do to others what you would have them do to you." In keeping with that he was planning to incorporate into his message I John 3:17, "If anyone has material possessions and sees his brother in need, but has no pity on him, how can the love of God be in him." Bob realized that this would speak directly to his own children, and wrestled with the decision to preach his planned sermon. But then he realized that if it was wrong to pick a scripture just to address a failing in someone with whom he had a difference, it was even more wrong to avoid a scripture because it might offend someone. His children were aware that he was in this series, and even though the passage spoke directly to them, their father was not "picking on" them but was following his consistent preaching program. As he pondered the issue, Bob believed that nothing less than the providence of God was involved in his scheduled plan to preach this sermon at a time when it so aptly applied to a situation in his own family.

Bob had always believed that in his sermon preparation nothing was more important than prayer. Yet as he was preparing for the following Sunday he prayed more fervently than ever. Therefore, he preached the sermon he had previously prepared, and asked God to make that sermon helpful to the whole congregation, but especially to speak to the attitude he had, with such disappointment, witnessed in his own children.

As they sat at the table for their noonday meal after the worship service that Sunday there was a strained and awkward silence. The usual warm family chatter was lacking. Bob and Karen were both aware that the children were still struggling with the possibility of their parents adopting two children. Bob wondered if his message had further alienated his sons and daughters from him.

Then from Ruth the tears and words exploded together. Her pent-up emotions erupted in a sudden outburst. "Dad and Mom," she sobbed. "I'm so sorry I was so selfish. I realize what a need there is in the lives of Ramón and Ramona, and how much you two want to help that family. I've thought and prayed about it a lot these past few days, and I know that my first reaction was not at all what God would want. I would gladly move into Esther's room with her, or share my room with Ramona."

Immediately Esther agreed, and asked Bob and Karen to forgive her earlier self-centered reaction. Phillip and Steven also got on board with the plan. Steven said, "Phillip and I have talked about it, and we still don't think you and Mom should give up your room. We would gladly sleep in bunk beds if you were to put a single bed in our room. Our room is large enough for that."

Bob and Karen choked back the tears at they clasped their hands in gratitude. Whether or not the adoption worked out, they had seen a thrilling spiritual maturing taking place in their children.

Through phone calls, mail and email the preparations were made for the adoption of Ramón and Ramona. Theresa had said that even though the heartbreak would be severe, she still thought it best that her two children come to America and become a part of the Morganton family. When Bob and all his family arrived in Haiti on their next annual trip the legalities to complete the adoption were worked out. When Ramón and Ramona were told of this, they ran to Karen and Bob with outstretched arms. But before they reached them, Phillip had scooped Ramón up in his arms, and Ruth had done the same to Ramona.

The Morganton's trip to Haiti always coincided with Dr. Moreland's visit there. Having learned of the adoption plan he told Theresa that he had arranged for her to be flown to the United States four times a year to visit her son and daughter. She glowed with joy at the news and said, "Thank you Doctor. That will ease the pain in my heart a lot when it comes time to say good-bye to my children."

Yet the pain of the separation was crushing. At the airport when the children felt the reality of leaving their mother, they wept uncontrollably. Theresa was holding Ramona, and said to her, through her own tears, "Honey, your mother will come to see you in just a few weeks." "How long is a week?" Ramona asked. "Just seven days," her mother answered. "That's a lot of days, Mommy," said Ramona. "I know it is." said Theresa,

"But you be a good girl for Mr. and Mrs. Morganton, and Jesus will make the time go quickly for you."

The early days with the Morganton's were difficult for Ramón and Ramona. They were obedient, Karen sometimes thought too compliant, to everything Bob and Karen said. They did not call Bob and Karen Mom and Dad, but Mr. and Mrs. Morganton. Bob and Karen did not mind this as they wanted the children to keep a warm and unique relationship with their birth mother. They still had their shy smiles, but seldom laughed.

The sadness became more evident in the evenings. The practice of the Morganton's had been to close the day with a time of devotions. This was not every evening because Bob's ministerial responsibilities and the children's school activities often interfered. Karen also had frequent evening responsibilities at the school, where she had taken a position as the school nurse, and also spent some time doing substitute teaching. Still most evenings the family would gather in the living room where one of them would read a short passage of Scripture. Sometimes they would sing a hymn and close with a prayer circle. After Ramón and Ramona had become a part of the family, Bob would take Phillip, Ruth, Steven and Esther with him into the living room, and Karen would take Ramón and Ramona into the den where she would read to them from a children's Bible story book.

When evening devotions were over, Ruth or Esther would take Ramona to her bed in Esther's room, and tuck her in bed. Phillip or Steven would take Ramón to the upper bunk in their room, in which Ramón had insisted he sleep, and tuck him in. As they were leaving her room Ruth and Esther would often hear Ramona say, "I want my

Mommy." Some nights they would hear both Ramón and Ramona sobbing themselves to sleep. This was heartbreaking to the family.

This evening sobbing grew less frequent, and finally stopped after a few weeks. Just after Ramona had turned three years old, Karen was walking by Esther and Ramona's bedroom. She heard a happy giggle, and turned and stood in the doorway. Esther was sitting on her bed, with one arm around Ramona. On her lap was a coloring book. As Karen looked at the girls, and when they looked back at her Ramona's face was beaming, and she said, "Momma, my sister is silly." Karen's heart leaped for joy at the words "Momma" and "sister." Then through her giggles Ramona said, "Ducks don't have ears, and cows don't have wings."

Karen walked to the girls and looked at the coloring book. On a picture of a duck Esther had drawn and colored rabbit's ears, and on a cow, large wings. Ramona pointed to them and again said, "Isn't Esther silly?" "Yes, your sister really is silly," said Karen. She turned and walked from the room, with tears of gratitude filling her eyes. She breathed a whispered prayer, "Thank you Father, for making our family a real family."

After the thorns of their birth children's early resentment, and the initial sorrow of Ramón and Ramona's move from their mother, roses began to bloom in abundance. Theresa had made two trips to the United States to visit her son and daughter. The reunions were always joyous, but her departure to return to Haiti always tearful. Then one day Karen came home from the school into Bob's study. She was bursting with excitement. "Bob," she said, "have you heard that Mr. Falcon, the school custodian is retiring?" Although he was minister of the church that sponsored the school, Bob had not heard that. Karen went on. "He just told us at our lunch break. Do you think that might be a perfect opportunity for

Theresa? She is an honest person, and a hard worker. I believe she could handle the job well."

"I'm as excited as you are about that possibility," Bob answered, "But it's not mine to decide; it will be up to the Board of Directors of the school."

"Yes, I know that," Karen responded. "But you will suggest that to them, won't you?"

"Certainly," Bob said. "Although it's not a big paying job, it would be more than she makes in Haiti, and it would make it possible for her to be near her children."

The school Board of Directors had a lengthy discussion about Bob's suggestion. They saw the benefits to Theresa and her family, but were concerned that Theresa was an unknown quantity. After considerable deliberation they decided to hire Theresa on a probationary basis, she would be salaried for a three month trial period, and then a decision would be made about permanent employment. With travel for Theresa already promised by Dr. Moreland, Bob quickly agreed to this arrangement.

When the word got to Theresa, she was thrilled to the core of her being. Yet she had her apprehensions. The position involved being on site five days a week for normal custodial duties. Once a month there was a heavy custodial and deep cleaning day. Grateful parents of the students who attended the school came to voluntarily do this work. Theresa felt confident about the routine custodial work, but she did have a real apprehension about organizing and supervising the monthly work days. After all, she was from a different country and of a different race than those she would be supervising. Therefore, it was with considerable trepidation that she accepted the offer to come to Rockview and work on a probationary basis with the school. She spent the month between the time she had accepted the offer until the date she was to come to the United States in frequent and fervent prayer.

Under the two week direction of Mr. Falcon before his retirement, Theresa quickly learned of her daily responsibilities. She was alert and energetic, and Mr. Falcon felt comfortable about his replacement. He did give her guidance in planning the first volunteer work day, and remained with her throughout that day. The volunteers showed some surprise when they learned that Theresa was to oversee their work. There were some rough spots in the coordination of the work, and through the day the volunteers continued to go to Mr. Falcon for guidance rather than ask Theresa. That night Theresa prayed for a long time that the Lord would help her do her work a bit better. She realized that her opportunity to remain near her children was dependant upon that job.

In the following month the staff of the school came to appreciate Theresa for her energy, her cheerfulness, and her obvious joy and gratitude to have an opportunity to get this job on a full time basis. When the volunteer work day came the following month, things went much more smoothly. At the close of the day there was warmth and a feeling of genuine fellowship between Theresa and the volunteers. After the third month, when the Board of Directors met it was a unanimous vote that Theresa be hired on a full time basis.

That evening at the home of the Morganton's there was a jubilant celebration with Bob, Karen, Theresa and all six children.

Theresa had acquired a small, one bedroom efficiency apartment. It was comfortable enough for her, but not large enough for her to have the children live with her. However, she was with them nearly full time. She ate lunch with them in the school cafeteria. Many evenings she came to the Morganton's for the evening meal. Some evenings she stayed late enough to tuck her son and daughter in bed.

It turned out to be a beautiful situation. Bob and Karen were the legal parents of Ramón and Ramona, but their birth mother was able to be with them on an almost full time basis. The two families had blended into one in a way Bob, even with his firm conviction of the providence of God, never could have imagined.

Bob had been quite athletic, and this ability was inherited by his children. Ruth and Esther both played on the high school varsity tennis team. Phillip was a first baseman on the baseball team, and Steven was an all conference point guard on the school basketball team. As Bob and Karen crept (it seemed more like ran) into their more mature years they enjoyed supporting their children and their teams in the athletic endeavors. Yet it was Ramón whose athletic ability really amazed them. He had been of slight build as a child, and in adolescent years kept his slender build but grew tall. At six foot five he had made the state all star team as a forward in basketball. Several colleges offered him scholarships, and it was a blessing that he was able to attend a good college because of his basketball prowess.

All six of the children enjoyed music. All of them sang in high school choruses, and Esther and Ramona played in the high school band.

After high school Phillip went to Hampton University to study architecture, and Steven enrolled in the local Junior College to study Business Administration. Ruth majored in secondary education and became a teacher right after graduation. Esther and Ramona, probably to a great degree influenced by their admiration of their mother, went into nursing. Ramón went to a state university and became a coach upon graduation. Bob and Karen took delight in watching as their children, both natural and adopted, grow up into responsible and effective citizens. Theresa also took great pleasure in how things had worked out for her children. She never ceased thanking God for the events that brought first her children, then her, into the United States.

The ministry continued to flourish, and often brought unexpected joys. One Sunday as Bob was seated on the platform during the song service he saw a familiar looking man enter the worship area. The man, now obviously in his retirement years was balding. He was rather short and stocky and had a round, pleasant face. His wife, a petite lady, and a younger man and wife were with him. The younger couple also had a child with them. Bob knew he was not a member of the congregation, but his appearance was so familiar Bob reached back in his memory to recall who this might be. Just before he rose to preach, it came to him. This was Norman Wilson, the prison guard whom Bob had led to be baptized during his incarceration.

As soon as the service ended, Bob rushed to him, embraced him, and invited Norman and his guests to come to dinner with him. Norman said, "Bob, I had to come and see you again, and introduce my wife and family to you. I want you to know how much you changed my life. This is my son Gregory, his wife and my grandson. I don't suppose you recall that time I came to you for advice about Gregory. What you told me about the responsibilities I had to be the spiritual leader of my family changed my life, and consequently my family's lives, dramatically. Gregory became a much more serious student. In fact he graduated with honors, went to college, and is now an engineer. I have become an elder in my local church, and although I have retired from my work as a prison guard, and their personnel has changed a lot, I still sometimes travel with the prison quartet which you helped get started. I thank the Lord (and then Norman laughed as he said) that God sent you to the prison where I was a guard.

"I do too, Norman. I really do" Bob said as he placed his arm around Norman's shoulders.

A similar thing happened on another occasion. Another man, younger but with an appearance and a mannerism that was so familiar Bob realized he knew that man. His wife and a girl appearing to be in her early teens, were with him. Bob again delved into his memory to try to place this young man. As he rose to preach his mind was still searching, but had found no answer. He managed to get the matter out of his mind and concentrate on his sermon. To Bob's surprise at the conclusion of his message this man, his wife, and the girl with them, stepped into the aisle and came forward in response to the invitation Bob had extended. As they came forward, and Bob got a close look into the man's face, he realized who this was. It was Glen Markle, the young man who had been convicted of child molestation, and also had come to Christ as a result of Bob's influence in prison. As he reached the front of the building, Bob extended his hand and gave Glen a warm handshake. Glen quickly told him why he had come forward. "Brother Bob," he said. "I came forward to thank you again for what you did for my life when you led me to Christ. I wanted to do it publicly, and testify about what a difference Christ has made in my life." He then told the congregation about how as a teenager he had been a child molester, and had justly been imprisoned for his crimes. He related the story of how Bob had introduced him to Jesus. After he had served his time he got a degree in counseling, married the lovely girl now standing with him, and became a counselor for those trapped by addictions. As Glen introduced Bob to his wife and daughter, Bob wiped his dampening eyes, and noticed how many in the congregation also lifted hands or handkerchiefs to the their eyes.

In his closing prayer Bob thanked God for what He had done in Glen's life, and for the wonderful way in which He continually brought good out of those things which many would consider far from good circumstances.

But things had not always been roses during these years. While the ministry continued to flourish, there were times when thorns among the roses were piercing, times when events Bob and Karen faced were filled with challenges and sometimes heartache.

THE STRUGGLES OF STEVEN

Some of the painful, thorny times that Bob and Karen went through during their more mature years had to do with Steven. During his years at the local community college, Bob and Karen began to detect the smell of cigarette smoke in Steven's hair and on his clothes. Bob and Karen and all the rest of the family have always been total abstainers from both alcohol and tobacco. They asked him if he had begun to smoke, and he said, "No, but I pick up that odor from the pool parlor. The place is blue with smoke."

It was then that Bob and Karen learned that he had been going with some of his college buddies to Pauley's Pool Parlor almost every afternoon when his classes were over. Bob knew that alcohol was served at the pool parlor, and he was concerned about that. He asked Steven if he thought that was the best environment for him to be in.

Steven answered, "Dad, don't be a Pharisee! You remember that Jesus was criticized for eating with publicans and sinners, and He pointed out to His accusers those were the very people who needed Him most." Steven went on: "Dad, I don't believe you understand what it's been like for my brother, my sisters and me. You know it's not the easiest thing in the world to be a P.K. (Preacher's Kid). Everybody looks at us like we are from another world. They all seem to think we have a "holier than thou" attitude; that we think we are better than everyone else. I've decided that I'm not going to live that

THE STRUGGLES OF STEVEN

way. I'm not going to be afraid to spend time with publicans and sinners."

Bob retorted, "You're right, Steven. I am not a P.K., but your mother was. I don't think you see any of those attitudes of self righteousness in her, do you?"

"Well, maybe not," said Steven, "but I've decided I'm not going to live my life in a bubble. But as I said, I'm not smoking or drinking, and I'm not going to let the lifestyle of the people there influence me. Maybe I can have a good influence on them."

"I hope you can, Steven," Bob answered. "But remember Paul said 'Don't be deceived, bad companions corrupt good morals.' "I know that," Steven replied. "But I know what I believe, and I'm not going to let other people lead me astray."

Bob did not argue with Steven about this, but he and Karen prayed regularly that Steven might have a greater influence on the crowd at the pool parlor than they were having on him.

Around the house, the family could not help but notice how frequently Steven kept referring to Kim. Finally one day Karen said, "Say Steven, who is this Kim?"

She's a friend I've made in class," Steven answered. Karen said, "She must be very good friend," responded Karen. "You speak of her often."

"Yes she is," said Steven. "I've really grown quite fond of her."

"Why don't you invite her to our house for dinner some evening soon?" replied Karen. "If you're that fond of her we'd like to meet her, and you may want her to meet your family."

"That's swell, Mom," said Steven. "I'd like to do that. I'm sure you'll like her."

The following Friday evening Steven brought Kim to dinner. She was a delightful girl; cheery, vivacious, and attractive. She spoke with a warmth that immediately made you feel comfortable around her. All the family immediately felt drawn to her - as if she had been a part of the family.

However, Bob and Karen detected the smell of tobacco, not only on her clothing and hair, but also on her breath. They also both thought that even though she must have tried to hide it with some kind of a mouth wash, they detected a hint of alcohol on her breath. During the conversation of the evening, they learned that she was the daughter of Ben Pauley, the owner of the pool hall. It was because of her that Steven had first begun to go to the pool parlor.

As time went on, Bob and Karen grew more concerned about Steven's relationship with Kim, and with the fact that Steven went to the pool hall almost every evening. They decided that even though Steven was now twenty, he was living in their house, and they should speak with him about their concerns. When they did, Steven at first was defensive, and Bob was obviously irritated. However as their conversation continued. both of them mellowed a bit.

"As for Kim," Steven said, "I'm growing more and more fond of her - in fact I may be falling in love with her. You have to admit, she is an extremely winsome young lady."

"I can't deny that," Bob said.

Karen spoke up, "But Steven, is she the girl you want to spend the rest of your life with? I think you will agree that her values are different from ours."

"They may have been and perhaps still are. But, Mom and Dad, she has grown up in a family far different from ours. There is much good in her which I see, but I don't believe you have seen yet. She really has a depth and a compassion for people that is not evident until you get to know her pretty well."

THE STRUGGLES OF STEVEN

"As for the pool hall, what is so bad about playing pool?" Steven continued.

"Well, I don't know if the game itself is all that bad, but the reputation of pool halls is not that good," was Bob's reply. "I know there's drinking and gambling that goes on there."

Steven became a bit excited as he answered, "Dad, let's think about this a little. I know you love playing golf and say that's alright, and jokingly call it a 'holey game,' and then you jest it's much better than croquet, which no one questions, and you call it a 'wicket game.' But think about this a moment. You play a game where the object is to take clubs and strike a ball into a hole. Pool is a game where you take cues and try to direct balls into pockets on the side and ends of the table. I don't see any difference in the moral or spiritual implications of the games"

"I have to admit you have a point" Bob said. "But it's the environment that bothers me. There is so much drinking and gambling in the pool hall."

Steven retorted, "Dad, do you claim that no one plays for money on the golf course? Why you yourself and your buddies played for a penny a hole. And were there not those who would order a beer in the club house after they finished their eighteen holes? I know that neither you nor any of your golfing partners drank, but there are also several of my friends who play at the pool parlor who do not drink a drop."

Steven went on: "Dad, if it's the environment that concerns you, why not change it? The church has that big recreation building that we only use once or twice a week. I do enjoy playing pool; why not put a pool table in the church recreation hall? We've already got a couple of ping pong tables in there. I don't see any difference between that and a pool table."

The suggestion struck an adverse cord in Bob. His immediate reaction was, "Son, I don't believe that's a good idea." However in the coming days as he thought over what Steven had said, he saw more and more logic in it. One night as they were lying in bed he said to Karen, "Honey, what do you think of what Steven said about a pool table in the church recreation hall?"

Karen answered, "You really can't fault his logic. He made quite a point about it not being spiritually or morally different from golf. His idea might have some merit."

Bob thought about the idea for several days. Then he decided that he would bring the idea to the eldership of the church. It was met with quite a wide difference of opinion by the elders. They decided to table the matter for a month, and then discuss it again. Bob then realized that the best person to present the idea was Steven, for after all he had dramatically changed Bob's thinking about the matter. The following month Steven was invited to the elder's meeting to present his perspective on the matter. No final decision on the pool table was made at that meeting, but it was decided to include it in another plan with which the leadership had been wrestling. With the growth of the congregation there had been consideration and discussion for several months about adding another person to the staff of the church. Just what would be the job description of the new staff member was still undetermined.

All the staff members of the church had been called with the understanding that the primary purpose of the church was to make disciples, and to nurture them in the Lord so that they in turn might lead others to Christ. The music minister, the education minister, the youth minister, the family life minister and all other employees of the church understood this and were committed to the concept. This had been a major factor in the steady growth of the congregation.

The family life minister in particular had found his work load getting heavier and heavier as the church had grown. It was decided that they would call another staff member to work in cooperation with the family life minister. His major work would be in the area of planning the recreational activities of the congregation. Thus he would be directing the programs of the recreation hall of the building. His title would be "Re-Creational" minister. His job description included helping new creatures in Christ to grow in their relation to the Lord, and to reach out to others to lead them to the experience of new birth in Christ. A recent Bible college graduate, Russell (Rusty) Richards, was interviewed, and he whole heartedly bought into the evangelistic concept of the program and was called to fulfill that ministry.

With the decision to call someone to this ministry it was agreed to add a pool table, a carpet ball table, an air hockey table and other such recreational things to the ping pong tables already in the recreation hall. The new Re- Creation minister entered his work with gusto, and the results were positive. Monday, Tuesday, Thursday and Saturday nights the Re-Creation hall was opened. The community soon learned of the program, and the participation was better than anyone had anticipated.

One of the things the Re-Creational minister did was have a craft class in which placards were made for the wall. They said such things as "No Profanity in This Building; Jesus is Listening," and "No Alcohol or Tobacco, Your Bodies are Temples of the Holy Spirit." It was amazing how the language of some whose speech was quite "spicy" when they first came to the Re-Creation center cleaned up after a couple weeks.

At Pauley's Pool Parlor there had always been rock and roll music playing At the Re-Creation center there was Gospel music, some contemporary and some traditional, always playing. At Pauley's

Pool Parlor that bar was always open; at the Re-Creation center there were snacks, fruit juices and soft drinks available on a donation basis. For the first couple of months this part of the program was a cost to the church, but after a few months the donations increased enough to meet the expenses.

Four times a year the quartet from the state penitentiary, the Inmate Angelois, came to sing in the Re-Creation hall. Although he no longer traveled with them, Norman Wilson would come for these concerts about twice a year. When the quartet came chairs were carried in from other parts of the building. After the first year the crowds for the appearances of the quartet got so large they had to change the venue to the worship auditorium.

On the nights the Re-Creation center was open to the public they would close the building at 11 P.M. However, at 10:45 all games were stopped, and the people gathered for a brief devotional and prayer time. This was usually led by Rusty, the Re-Creational minister, but sometimes Bob or one of the other ministerial staff would lead it. Many folk would leave when time came for these devotions, but Rusty and the rest of the staff were pleased to see an increasing number were staying to the end of devotions.

Steven was going to Pauley's Pool Parlor less frequently and was at the Re-Creation center many of the nights it was open. Kim was with him. Kim was one of those whose previously rather "spicy" speech cleaned up considerably after a few visits to the Re-Creation center.

Kim came to the home of the Morganton's more and more often. Bob remarked to Karen one evening that they had seen a considerable change in her. No longer was the odor of tobacco or alcohol on her. One evening she said to them: "Mr. and Mrs. Morganton I want to thank you for making me feel so welcome.

It's certainly different here than it is in my home. I see now where all the wonderful characteristics I see in Steven came from. There is a certain serenity here that I have not seen either in my home or any other. And you know, I see how much fun folk are having at the Re-Creation center. I'm going to talk to my dad about stopping the sale of alcohol at his pool parlor. Obviously you don't need that stuff to have a good time."

Bob and Karen's uneasiness about Kim had been decreasing in recent weeks, and now it completely melted away.

During these years Phillip had secured an excellent job with an architectural firm in a city about an hour and a half's drive from Rockview. Soon after his move there he married Rose, and within a matter of little over a year they started their family. Within five years they had three children. They returned often to Rockview to visit Bob and Karen, who enjoyed their grandchildren tremendously. Ruth was hired as a teacher, also some distance away from Rockview. She married and in a few years had two children. Like Phillip and Rose she and her husband and the children made frequent trips to Rockview to visit her parents. Esther was employed as a nurse for a local doctor. She had not been there long when she married the doctor and they in a few years were the parents of three sons and a daughter. It was indeed a joyous, and somewhat boisterous, occasion when the children and grandchildren came to visit Bob and Karen. At least once a year the family all planned to come home at one time. On those occasions they rented the facilities at a church camp. Theresa, Ramón and Ramona joined them on these occasions. As years went by, Ramón and Ramona each married, and brought their children with them. These occasions were to Bob and Karen, as well as to many others of the family, the highlight of their year.

THE STRUGGLES OF STEVEN

There was a great amount of musical talent in this extended family. Several of them played musical instruments. These family reunions included a great amount of singing. From Phillip, Esther, and Ruth's families an octet had been formed that became quite accomplished. They frequently sang at churches and at other functions throughout the area. Sometimes the personnel in the octet varied, but always the quality remained high. One of the numbers they performed was the Hallelujah Chorus from Handel's Messiah. The octet had developed their rendition of this to the point that they sounded like a full choir. At nearly every concert they performed, this number was requested.

Steven completed his degree in business administration, and he and Kim married. Steven was not a CPA, but he had taken several courses in accounting. He was hired at a good salary by a Real Estate Development company in Rockview. This company was growing, and were involved in developing several large planned communities around the state. Steven was skilled in his work, and advanced quickly with the company. The time came when his work took him out of town for several days at a time. This may have been the factor that contributed to some of the heartache Bob and Karen faced in the following years.

Kim became pregnant, but miscarried in her fifth month. Two years later, Bradley was born to Steven and Kim. He was a Downs Syndrome child. Then in another two years Susan was born. She was an absolutely beautiful baby, a blue-eyed blond. As a toddler she showed the charm and vivaciousness of her mother. She was quick to win the hearts of everyone who saw her. Many remarked that she reminded them of Shirley Temple, and some folk even dubbed her "Little Shirley."

Steven kept getting promotions in his job. This also meant more and more time away from home. Kim became concerned that Steven may be spending more nights away than were really necessary. There was an attractive young woman that the development company sometimes sent to the same assignment on which Steven had been sent. Kim could not help but be concerned when Steven would call the day he was scheduled to come home and say he would have to stay for another day.

One evening Kim and Bradley were at Bob and Karen's home. Bob and Karen had noticed that Kim had seemed distracted and worried. She looked tired. Bob slid his arm around his daughter-in-law's shoulder, and said, "Kim, you haven't been yourself lately. You look distraught and tired. Is anything wrong? Is there anything we can help you with."

Kim's chin began to tremble. Her eyes moistened. "Dad," she said. "I've tried not to let it bother me, and not to say anything to any one about it, but I'm concerned about Steven. I know I should trust him, but I can't help worrying when he stays away longer and longer than I think he should on his business trips. He often travels with that young attractive woman with whom he works. When he is home he seems restless and irritable. He still loves the children, and is so sweet with Susan. As soon as he gets home, she runs to him, and he'll spend the whole evening holding her on his lap. But he pays less and less attention to me. He is not nearly as affectionate as he used to be. You know Steven has always been a total abstainer, but lately when he comes home his breath smells heavily of cloves or mints or something else as though he is trying to mask some other smell on his breath."

By now Kim was sobbing uncontrollably. "Mom and Dad, I don't know what to do. I want to trust Steven, I don't want to nag, but I must admit I am deeply concerned."

Kim laid her head on her father-in-law's shoulder, and wept. Karen stepped to the other side of her, and the three embraced in an effort to comfort Kim. "Honey," said Bob, "Let's not jump to conclusions. I understand your deep concern, and Karen and I are also deeply troubled by what you are saying. I would advise you to keep up your attempt to not talk about this, and to trust Steven as much as you possibly can. He does have a highly stressful job, and his restlessness and irritability at home may be a part of that job. I would suggest that for the present time you continue to be the best wife to him that you possibly can be. Keep praying for him, and Karen and I will also keep both you and Steven in our prayers every day."

Even though she was so deeply concerned about Steven, Kim's spiritual life deepened week by week. She made a personal commitment to Christ, and became an active member of the church at Rockview. She began teaching in the pre-school department of the Sunday school, and was deeply loved by the children and their parents. She was a regular participant in the ladies' group and the mid-week Bible studies. Her interest in learning Scripture and her excited personal witness about Christ was obvious to all the church membership. The congregation often commented to Bob and Karen, "You must be awfully proud of your daughter-in-law."

However, Steven's participation with the church grew less and less. He attended most Sundays, but his activity in the church did not go beyond that. Many weekends, to the dismay of Kim, Steven did not come home from his business trips.

One morning when Susan was eighteen months old she slept well beyond her usual wake-up time. Kim became concerned, and went in and placed her hand on Susan's forehead. She detected a fever, and Susan stirred slightly, opened her eyes just a tiny slit, and then fell back to sleep. Kim left the room, but in less than an hour went back and picked Susan up out of her bed. Her little body felt limp, and Kim carried her into the living room and sat down with Susan on her lap. Her maternal instincts soon made her realize that something was not right with her little girl, so she went to the hospital emergency room with her. The attending doctor, Dr. Norris, happened to be in the admission room, and saw Kim carrying Susan in. His eyes happened to land upon Susan, and he saw something that obviously concerned him. He told Kim to bring her straight into the examination room. In a few minutes he turned to Kim with obvious consternation. "Mrs. Morganton," he said, "Your daughter has the symptoms of meningitis. I'm going to have her admitted immediately to the pediatric ward of the hospital. Has Susan had any flu-like symptoms in the last few days?"

"Yes," Kim answered. "About two weeks ago she was fussy and said her head hurt. I gave her a baby aspirin, put her to bed, and in just a few hours she seemed to be fine."

"That fits a pattern," responded the doctor. "There is an H strain flu virus that will have that kind of an effect, but in a few days, even though there are no further symptoms, can infect the meninges, the membranes that envelope the brain and the spinal cord. I must tell you Mrs. Morganton, that this is a serious condition. I would advise you to call your husband and tell him his daughter is critically ill."

Kim immediately called Steven, and he said he would start home right away. Kim told him to come straight to the hospital. Steven ignored the speed limit, and arrived at the hospital just before nightfall. He found Kim and Susan in an isolated hospital room; Kim wearing a surgical mask and a protective gown. Steven was made to put on the same gear before he was allowed in the room. By this time, Susan had slipped into a deep coma, and hadn't responded at all for several hours. Bob and Karen had come to the hospital and were keeping vigil in a waiting room in the pediatric ward of the hospital. Several other people from the Rockview church were there. One of them asked Dr. Norris how things looked for little Susan. "Not good," the doctor answered. "Fewer than one out of five, who have incubated this kind of virus for as long as Susan has, survive. We are treating her with a cocktail of antibiotics, and hoping for the best. The next twenty four hours will tell the story, but I would be surprised if she survives till morning." Steven and Kim were not told of that conversation, but came to learn of it later.

Late that evening the doctor came to the window of Susan's isolated room, and motioned for Steven and Kim to come out. He said to them, "You folks can do nothing for your daughter by waiting here. I advise you to go home and get some rest. Please do that, and come back in the morning. In the meantime, I and my staff are doing everything we can for your little girl."

Kim and Steven took off their masks and gowns, and left them in a designated place there to be discarded. They went to the waiting room, where Bob and Karen and the others from the church were waiting. When the church members saw them, they expressed their concern, assured Steven and Kim of their prayers, and left. When they were gone, Bob came to his son, and said, "Steven, I know this is a terribly difficult time for you, and it may be hard for you to realize it now, but remember, 'all things work together for good to those who love God, to those who are ....

"Stop it Dad, just stop it," Steven almost shouted. "I've heard you say that all my life, and I just can't believe it any longer. I think you're living in a dream world."

Bob was so shocked he was speechless. So Steven continued. "Dad, you've said that all your life. But think about it for a while. You have always tried to serve God, but look what's happened to you.

Your first wife, whose pictures I've seen many times, was a beautiful and I understand extremely talented woman. Yet she was taken from you in the prime of life. Then add to that the fact that you were accused of her murder, and served prison time for that. Those don't sound like good things to me."

Bob regaining his composure since his initial shock at Steven's remarks, now responded. "Yes, I agree that in themselves these were not 'good things.' But the Bible doesn't say all things are good. It says that all things work together **for** good. That's the amazing thing about it. God is able to orchestrate all things, both good and bad things, together for those who love Him. Steven, do you realize that if Kathy had not died, I would not have married your mother, and you wouldn't even exist? Yes, Kathy was a beautiful and talented woman, and I found it hard to accept when Kathy was killed in that accident, and it was even harder to accept when I was judged guilty for her death, and imprisoned. But at that time I continued to believe that all things work together for good because the Bible says it, and because I had seen it demonstrated in other's lives. However, in the years to follow I came to experience personally how wonderfully true that promise is. My prison experience equipped me for the years of ministry to follow in a way I never would have believed if I had not experienced it myself. God used those years to bring about some undeniably good things in the prison. God used my limited talents to help develop a prison quartet that has won wide acclaim. There were those converted there whose lives have had a tremendous impact for the cause of Christ. No, Kathy's death and my imprisonment in and of themselves would not have been good things, but in the hand of God they were used for tremendous good."

"But Dad," Steven contended, "consider how much more I have prospered than you have. You have always been faithful, you have served God without wavering. A twelve or fourteen hour work day was the rule more than the exception for you. And what have you got to show for it? I know you have a large and comfortable house, due in the main to your own labor on it. In contrast to that, although I am away several days a week, I have never put in the long hours that you did. And although your house is comfortable enough, it is not worth half as much as mine. I have several acres, a swimming pool, and amenities far beyond those in your house. I drive a new top of the line car every two years. I can travel or vacation anywhere in the world I want. Can't you see that in spite of your life-long conviction that all things work together for good to those who love God, I have been more richly blessed that you have?"

A second shock wave struck Bob. In response he said, "Steven, how can you measure God's blessing by material things? My life has been filled with joy and blessings that far exceed the value of houses or acres of land or cars or any other material things."

But Steven retorted, "And Dad, if all things work together for good, how can you explain what's happened to me. We lost our first child at birth, our second child, Bradley, has Down's Syndrome, and now after we finally had this beautiful, precious daughter, God is taking her away from us. How can that be the act of a loving God who is working things out for our good?"

Placing his hand on Steven's shoulder, and keeping it there even though Steven flinched as though trying to draw away, Bob said, "Son, you are in the midst of some things that are not good. But if you live a normal life span it's not yet even half-time in your life. Let God's purpose work out in your life. Don't conclude that Susan isn't going to survive. Those people who were in this waiting room have all said they would pray for her, and I know that some of them have called believers over an area of several states and asked them to pray fervently for Susan, and for you and Kim and Bradley. Although the medical prognosis now is not good, I strongly believe in the power of prayer. I can't promise you that Susan will live through this, no one can guarantee that. That may not be God's will. But I do know that God knows the heartache you're experiencing now - after all He saw His own Son cruelly tortured and murdered. I know your sorrow touches His heart, and that He sympathizes with you. And I know that He is able to supply to you and Kim a peace that is beyond human understanding."

Bob went on, "And, son don't you recall what Kim told us about her uncle Charles? He was on a scaffold forty feet off the ground when a metal scaffold brace was being handed up to him, and he happened to get it too near a power line carrying between seven thousand and twenty thousand volts. An electrical charge arced from that power line into the scaffold brace and then into his body. He was knocked unconscious by the immense electrical charge, fell down on the scaffold, and then rolled off and fell forty feet to the ground. He landed on grass, flat on his back parallel to a huge concrete base just inches away that was the foundation for the structure which held up the sign which he was working on forty feet above. The doctors surmised that perhaps the shock had stopped his heart, and that when he hit the ground the jar started it again. They also noted that he had landed in the best position to avoid breaking or smashing his bones. A few days later after some time in the hospital Uncle Charles was polishing his car in his yard. An insurance adjuster came by and asked to see the man who had fallen from that scaffold by the lumberyard advertising sign. Charles said, 'That's me.' The insurance man's jaw dropped in amazement. He said 'I went to look at the sight of that fall, and the people there described what had happened, showed me from where you fell, and I wrote down on my initial report, TOTALLY

DISABLED. Now I come down here, and find you polishing your car. This is incredible." Within a few weeks, Charles was back on his construction job. (12)

"So," Bob continued. "God is awesome. He often brings deliverance out of situations that seem hopeless."

The hospital was quiet now, visitors had gone home. Steven and Kim stood for a few minutes looking through the window into the isolated room where the motionless body of their tiny daughter lay with numerous tubes running from various machines into her body. They embraced, shed silent tears, and left to go home. That night kneeling at their bedside with Kim, Steven, who had not prayed for a long time, turned to his Heavenly Father and said, "Lord, if you count us worthy parents, and if we can raise Susan in keeping with your will, we plead with you to let her live."

For the next day Steven and Kim stayed near the isolated room where Susan lay, still motionless. It was on the third day that little Susan stirred, and opened her eyes. In a couple of hours a nurse brought Susan to where Kim and Steven had been waiting. They placed Susan in Kim's lap. She was still wavering between consciousness and unconsciousness. Her eyes would open for a few seconds and then close again. Once, as they opened Steven held her favorite stuffed toy before her. A slight smile broke the unresponsive pattern of the last few days, and she weakly lifted an arm to reach for the toy. Steven would remark later, "Never has a weak smile or the struggled motion of an arm been so beautiful to me." Susan continued her improvement, and went on to live a full and productive life." (13)

STEVEN'S ZEALOUS RETURN

Although they may well have been, it was never learned for certain, whether or not Kim's fears of Steven's suspicious actions and perhaps even infidelity were justified. He never confessed anything about it. However, after Susan's amazing recovery, there was an obvious change in Steven's behavior and attitude. He began coming home every weekend. He no longer called to say he was going to have to stay away another day or so after his expected return home. His affectionate and caring attitude toward Kim returned. He once again attended worship with her regularly.

About three months after Susan's return home from the hospital, Steven went to Mr. Grundy, his boss, to tell him he was going to quit his job. This was a weighty decision as his annual salary had now grown to a six figure number. It was also a shocking revelation to his employer. His employer tried to persuade him to stay with the company, and told him that they would give him a sizable increase in his already generous salary. Steven thanked him but declined, saying, "No my mind is made up."

When Mr. Grundy asked him where he was going to work, Steven answered, "I don't know yet." Now his boss was totally perplexed. He exclaimed: "Steven, I don't understand this. You were doing well with our company; you are the best superintendent we have ever had, we have been pleased with your work, and we thought you

STEVEN'S ZEALOUS RETURN

were perfectly happy here. What in the world has happened; what makes you want to leave now, especially when you don't even have another job lined up?"

Steven answered, "It is nothing about the company. I have been re-evaluating my priorities, and decided to make some changes. I have not been spending nearly the time with my family that I should. Nearly losing my daughter made me realize what is really important in life, and I'm determined to give more attention to those things. I want to give you one month's notice. In the meantime I will wrap up the couple of projects I have got going, and will do my best to train and break in whomever you may choose to take my position." In spite of Mr. Grundy's efforts to change his mind, Steven stuck to his decision with resolution.

When Steven told Kim of his decision, her delight was obvious. However, her expression of joy soon turned to one of obvious consternation. "But Honey," Kim said. "What will you do? Do you have any other job lined up anywhere?" With a surprising unconcern Steven answered: "No, not yet, but I'm not worried. I gave Mr. Grundy a month's notice. While I have been on this job I have had several offers from other companies, and I know something is out there. We are well ahead on our mortgage payments and have a good bit of equity in our home. If need be we could refinance our house and cut monthly payments considerably. We have a pretty good nest egg in our savings account, and we could get by several months without employment. We may not be able to take the long oversees vacations we have in the past, but I have decided I would be just as happy spending part of my vacation time here at home with you and the kids and taking shorter trips to things nearer home."

Kim's eyes began to tear up, and she said "That sounds like music to my ears."

Steven went on: "Kim, I know I didn't talk this over with you before I tendered my resignation, and I apologize to you for that. But I have given much prayer to the matter. Dad has convinced me that to those who love God and are called according to His purpose, all things do work out for good. I admit that for the past few years I have given no thought to God's purpose for my life. Susan's near death made me think things over, and I'm going to start trying to live in keeping with God's purpose, no matter what that may be. Whatever employment I may find, I have determined that I am not going to work away from home most of the time like I did before, and I'm convinced that God will provide for my family even with a steep decrease in my salary. I hope you can live with my decision, although I did make it much too much on my own."

"Live with that?" Kim almost shouted. "Darling, you don't know how many of my prayers have just been answered."

Steven was right in that, as soon as the news got out that he was leaving the development company he had been with, job offers came in abundance. Many of them were quite attractive. However, most of these demanded that he be out of town a lot, which he had determined not to do. Steven gave them consideration, but had not decided on any of them.

Perhaps it was providential. Mayor Ted Meyers had served the city for over twenty years, and was extremely popular. After each term he had been re-elected by a landslide. However, he had come to the decision that it was time to retire, and had told the city council so. He suggested to them that the nature of the city was changing, and he recommended that they transition from a mayoral form of government to a city manager. The city manager would not be an elected official, but would be called by the city council, and would be under their oversight. This council would also have the power to fire the city manager.

The council consisted of five men and two women. They had advertised for a city manager, and had half a dozen interested and interesting applicants. However, they had settled on none of them. One of the men and one of the women on the council were members of the Rockview church. Knowing that Steven was transitioning from one job to another, they approached him one Sunday just after the morning worship had ended. They told him of the search for a city manager, of which Steven had been well aware, and asked him if there was any chance he would be interested in the job. They said if he were interested, they would present his name to the council for consideration.

The offer surprised, but also rather excited Steven. The following week he told them that he was not sure how interested he was, but if they wanted to submit his name for consideration, that would be alright with him. Within a few days Steven received a call from the chairman of the city council. Rather than submit a written application he asked him if he would come before the council for an interview. He said that they knew as much about Steven as they would learn from the written application, and preferred just to talk with him personally. They mentioned that since this was a new position for the city, they were not violating any protocol for filling the position, as none had been established as yet.

The interview went on for hours, and was extremely thorough. Steven shared his philosophy that government, to be the most effective, should be limited. He believed in building codes that would assure that any structure in the city be safe, solid and of quality material, but that some of the requirements of the code as it presently stood were unduly restrictive and needless. He said he was for taxes being as low as possible, but sufficient to provide capable, well trained and sufficiently salaried policemen and firefighters. He wanted to see the tax structures such that both present and future businesses were encouraged.

"We don't expect you to punch a clock," the chairman of the Council said. "If your work is in order, and you would like to take an afternoon, or a day off at your own discretion, we have no problem with that. In city hall there is a pool of secretaries, and you may make use of one, or any of them, as you have need."

"Again, we know that your salary will be a pittance in comparison to what you have been receiving, so I guess we are appealing to your sense of community service and the help we believe you would be to our city."

Within a few days the chairman of the city council called again. "Steven" he said. "It has been the unanimous decision of the city council to offer you the position of city manager, if you are willing to take it. Please let us know in a few days of your decision."

Steven told Kim of the call, and they spent a couple of days pondering the choice. As they had already made plans to reduce their cost of living in several areas and they thought that with careful planning, and even a bit more belt tightening they could "make do" on the salary. Steven saw it as an opportunity to commit himself to a purpose bigger than himself, a course which had been on his mind when he resigned from the development company. So Steven accepted the position as city manager, and the family made adjustments to an entirely new life style.

Not long after that "Rusty" Richards, the Re-Creational minister at the Rockview church was called to a preaching ministry at another congregation, and presented his resignation to the elders. They accepted it with regret, for Rusty had done a good work with them.

They told Rusty they were pleased with his acceptance of a preaching ministry, congratulated on being chosen by the congregation calling him, and assured him that he would have their continued love and prayer support.

Their search for a replacement proved difficult. Rusty had totally bought into the church's position that every member of the staff be committed to evangelism and discipleship. To find another so committed, they soon learned, was far from an easy thing to do.

When the time came for Rusty to make his move, the church still had not filled the position for a Re-Creational director for the congregation. Remembering the fact that the creation of the Re-Creational Center had been at the suggestion of Steven, the elders came up with the idea of asking him to fill the position on a temporary basis until they were able to find someone to do it full time. They offered him a small stipend each week if he would take that responsibility temporarily.

When Steven talked this over with Kim, she offered to be of help to him in any way she could. Realizing that the whole concept had been developed around the idea of family involvement, and that they, taking Bradley and Susan with them, could make two nights a week their nights to be at the Re-Creational Center to oversee things, decided they would assume responsibility to keep the Center open. This meant that the schedule for the Re-Creational Center would be reduced to two nights a week.

Bradley and Susan looked forward to these nights. Although Susan had to stand on a chair at one end of the carpet ball table to play, she and Bradley loved playing carpet ball.

Rusty Richards, being the thoughtful and thorough kind of person he was, had written a document which he called "Principles and Procedures for Operating the Re-Creational Center." Steven found these to be extremely helpful, and continued to operate the Center just as Rusty had.

Steven and Kim, in talking over the decision to take the position, had come to the conclusion that they would not accept even the small token stipend that had been offered them. As they had already decided to live on the reduced salary Steven was receiving, and as their work at the Re-Creational Center would mean no additional cost to them, they declined the offering for a stipend. The leadership of the church appreciated this, but insisted that if Steven and Kim had any financial stress come, they should let them know about it, and promised that they would gladly pay them the small salary that had been offered.

When people of the congregation learned of this, and realized the sacrifice Steven and Kim had made, two other couples came forward, each couple volunteering to be responsible for overseeing the activities of the Center one night a week. This meant that the Center could again stay open four nights week.

This program worked surprisingly well. It's success was not because Rusty was no longer needed, but because Rusty had done his job so well. The principles and procedures he had laid out, plus the wholesome and family-friendly atmosphere he had created had laid a foundation that was beneficial for any who would take the baton and carry on the work. His presence and leadership had created a spirit of cooperation and sacrifice among the people that lasted after he had left and made it possible for the work to carry on with volunteer leadership.

When the program using volunteers had gone on so well for a year, the leadership met to decide whether or not to continue their search for another salaried staff member to be the Re-Creational director. Those who were working on a volunteer basis were willing to continue. In fact, there had been other volunteers who had come forward to lend help. With things going so well, all those who had been volunteering were called into a meeting with the elders, deacons and staff of the church, and asked for their thoughts on the matter. Every one of them agreed that they were enjoying their participation, and in fact felt a satisfaction in feeling they were making a contribution to the witness of the church they had never experienced before.

It was Steven who suggested at that meeting: "I know that Andrew Matson, our Family Life minister, under whose direction we have been working, has incorporated into his work a ministry to single parents and their children. Most of these are regular participants in the activities of the Re-Creational Center and attend the worship services of the church. I also know that many of these are feeling extreme financial stress. I would suggest that, if these volunteers are willing, as they have indicated, to proceed in their present capacity, that the funds which had been designated to the employment of a Re-Creational Minister be designated to brother Matson, our Family Life Minister, to be used at his discretion, to aid those families."

Their was a resounding "Amen" to Steven's suggestion, and another new and dynamic ministry was added to the already effective witness of the Rockview church.

Steven and Kim budgeted carefully, but were finding it a challenge to meet monthly expenses. While they had once shopped at the most expensive and exclusive stores, Kim was soon comfortable shopping at thrift stores. She became an expert at finding excellent buys on used items. One day Steven said to Kim, "Honey, I know you budget carefully to handle the household expenses, and I have an idea that may make it easier. We have several acres that are presently just lawn, and are virtually unused. We still haven't used any of that "nest egg" I mentioned we had laid aside in case we really needed something.

I saw a pretty good small used tractor at Ben's Resale Warehouse the other day. It was for sale at a fraction of its original price. What would you think if we used a portion of our "nest egg" to buy it, and put in a couple of acres of vegetable garden. My work with the city allows me considerable free time, and although this would take an initial investment, over the years it would save us considerable in grocery expenses."

Kim was silent for a few moments. Then she answered, "Steven, although I have been aware that grocery prices are going up, and our costs are increasing as the children grow, my grasp on the suggestion you are making is pretty limited. You have much more knowledge about how that would work out than I do, and you know what your responsibilities to the city are. The idea sounds workable to me, but I'm going to leave that decision with you."

The next day Steven went to Ben's Resale Warehouse and bought the small tractor with attachments that would handle the little farming enterprise they were about to begin.

THE NEW VENTURE FLOURISHES

The decision to plant a garden proved to be a most propitious choice for the family. Steven found that he was able to well fulfill his responsibilities as City Manager in five or six hours a day, and to take days or afternoons off without interfering with his work. He found working with his hands to be enjoyable after so many months of being in occupations which were basically managerial. The fresh air and the manual work were invigorating for him. Kim also took an immediate interest in the project. She began to read agriculture journals and learned a good bit about developing rich and productive soil. Soon the two acres of garden were producing far more vegetables than the family could consume. They began sharing their produce with neighbors. These neighbors frequently commented that vegetables that Steven and Kim grew were as good as, or better, than any they could buy in local markets.

One day one of the neighbors to whom Steven and Kim had regularly been giving some of the produce said, "Steve, I feel bad about taking vegetables from you and paying you nothing. I would gladly pay you as much, or even more, than similar produce would cost me at the grocery store. Yours is every bit as good as any we could buy anywhere in the area, and to buy from you is much more convenient, since you are right here in my neighborhood. I insist on paying you a fair price. In fact, I think you ought to set up a booth right along the side of the road here to sell what you grow. I know you would have an instant clientele."

So after a brief discussion with Kim, the couple began a new enterprise. They put up a canvas awning, and set some tables under it to make a small vegetable sales booth. There was considerable traffic on the street that went past their garden, as it went into one of the better housing developments of the city. The neighbor was absolutely right. Quickly there was a considerable clientele developed to buy their produce. Two evenings a week, from 4 P.M. to about 5:30 P.M., the time when people going home from their jobs, past the produce stand, Kim or Steven would tend it. In those three hours a week they would usually sell all the produce they had grown.

One day, as they were picking beans in the garden, Steven said to Kim, "Honey, I want to thank you for the sacrifices you have made as we had adjusted to a much smaller income. You used to shop at the finest stores, now you shop at thrift stores. You used to buy vegetables at the store, now you work in the garden to grow our own. You used to have more leisure time for yourself, now you work in the garden or tend the produce stand. I want to know, are you as happy as when I was making a larger income?"

Steven's heart sank at her answer. Hoping that since he had more time at home, and their marriage and family life was stronger would have more than compensated for the financial loss they experienced, his spirit shriveled when Kim answered, "No, I am not."

Kim paused and witnessed the shock and disappointment on Steven's face. Then she went on. "Being 'as happy' infers being equally happy. Equally happy falls far short of describing the happiness I am now enjoying. Steven, words cannot explain how much more satisfied I am with our lives together now that you are home more. Yes, we have to skimp and deny ourselves some of the things we used to buy or enjoy without even a second thought. But those things are nothing compared to the joy I have with you and the family, or the pleasure it is to work with you on such things as this garden and the produce stand. Steven, I love you dearly, and honestly I have never been so happy in all my life."

Steven and Kim trampled three bean plants at they embraced in the middle of the garden and experienced a love and unity of spirit they had not felt for years.

Things went so well with the garden and the produce stand and the project was proving so fulfilling that Kim and Steven decided to expand it. With the small tractor he had bought, Steven plowed five more acres, and more vegetables, and some fruit trees and fruit bushes were planted. Bradley, their Downs Syndrome son, learned to operate the tractor. While she was a toddler, even Susan enjoyed working with the garden. When she helped Kim pick beans she couldn't understand why she couldn't pick the "baby beans" but had to allow them to grow to maturity before they harvested them. Other than the tractor the rest of the implements for the garden were hand tools. When they dug potatoes, Susan would give a shriek of delight when they dug into the hills and the potatoes would come rolling out.

Kim and Steven had worked lovingly with Bradley to help him function on the highest level possible. He had also attended a class for students with special needs at the school the church operated. He had learned some simple arithmetic and the alphabet. He was able to read at about a second grade level. Steven and Kim believed he was competent enough to help in the produce stand. They packaged their produce in one, five and ten dollar sizes to make it easier for Bradley to compute the price when he dealt with customers. Bradley soon learned to handle this quite well. In fact he became competent

THE NEW VENTURE FLOURISHES

enough that there were times when Kim and Steven left him in charge for thirty or forty minutes at a time.

One day, just a few minutes after Bradley had begun to tend the stand on his own, a car drove slowly by. Seeing several customers at the stand, it went on. It returned from the opposite direction, and again drove by slowly. Then the car returned and, seeing no customers there, stopped. A man and a woman got out of the car, and hurriedly picked one of the ten dollar containers of strawberries. Then they came to the table where Bradley was tending the cash register. The man pushed Bradley away, and the woman emptied the cash register in her purse. The man picked up the strawberries and the two hurried quickly to the car and drove away.

Bradley, able to recognize letters and numbers as he was, picked up a note pad beside the cash register and copied AMR472 from the license plate of the car. He then dialed 911 as his parents had taught him to do and told what had happened. Within five minutes a police car was there, and Bradley told them about the stolen strawberries and cash. One of the officers made another call, and within five minutes another police car, a K9 unit, was there.

By this time Steven and Kim had returned, and seeing the police cars were alarmed as they approached the produce stand. Bradley told his parents what had happened, and one of the officers said to Steven and Kim, "You can be mighty proud of this young man. He did exactly what he should have done. He may have helped us solve a case that we have been working on for months. There has been a rash of break-ins and robberies in this area. Sometimes the things stolen have been just petty larceny, but other times the thieves had taken things of considerable value; tools, jewelry, guns, cash and other things. Your son has given us the best lead we have had. There is a man and wife team whom we strongly suspect, but there has never been enough evidence to even get a search warrant for their property. This may be the break-through we have been hoping for."

The officers called the police station, and sure enough the license plate of the car coincided with the pair the police had suspected. With Bradley's information, they were able to quickly secure the search warrant they had long wanted. They drove to the address of the owners of the car, took the dog to the car which they now had legal right to open. The dog barked when he was led to the open car door, indicating he had recognized the odor of strawberries which he had sniffed back at the produce stand. With the search warrant they had, they then demanded entrance into the couples' house and garage. Thousands of dollars worth of jewelry, guns, tools and other items matching those reported stolen were found. Fortunately some of those who reported items stolen from them had recorded their serial numbers. The police where quickly able to identify these items, and the couple was arrested. The area newspapers carried an article entitled "**Downs Syndrome Young Man Helps Solve Serial Robbery Case.**" The news articles included a picture of Bradley and the police dog together. Bradley would beam with pride as customer after customer at the produce stand congratulated him.

Bradley was given a $1,000 reward which had been advertised for information leading to the arrest of those responsible for the numerous recent robberies in the area. Steven and Kim immediately created a fund for the care of Bradley when they would no longer be able to be responsible for him. This $1000 was placed into this account. Even though in their family there was a sense of contentment and happiness, Steven, ever since he had left his job with the development company, had been uneasy about the fact that they had not made any preparation for retirement years, or for Susan's college years. Perhaps this was the reason that their small vegetable farm and produce stand became so unexpectedly profitable. With profits beyond their expectations they were able to install an irrigation system. Even in years of drought, when the fruits and vegetables in the local markets were "slim pickins" Steven and Kim's garden was producing abundant crops. They did not hesitate to give continued thanks to the Lord of the Harvest for the profits they were experiencing. They attributed the success they were having with their small farming adventure to God rather than claiming it was their diligence or skills that so blessed them.

COMPASSION AND COURAGE

Steven's administrative abilities as City Manager proved a genuine benefit to the city. He was able to bring his vision of increased services without increased taxes to reality by appealing to the people of the city to respond to the same motive that had inspired him to take the job of City Manager. Through various programs and communications he appealed to their civic pride and personal involvement in the things that would benefit the community. He placed a great emphasis upon volunteerism. It was no secret to the city that Steven had sacrificed considerably for the welfare of the community by leaving his lucrative job to take the position of City Manager. His attitude of self-sacrifice and service was contagious. When an appeal was made for funds to expand and make considerable improvements to one of the city parks, a commercial enterprise in the city said they would sponsor that project if a sign could be placed in the park acknowledging their contribution. A service club in the city offered to take the maintenance of the park as one of their projects. Several other concerns and organizations followed suit, and soon Rockview was one of the most attractive and family friendly cities in the state.

In his capacity as City Manager, Steven had close contact with the police and judicial system. One day six young men were brought into court being tried for public disorderliness, destruction of property, and possession of a controlled substance. The six had been apprehended together and it was strongly suspected that they were a part of a gang, several of which had begun to make their appearance in the area. As Steven attended the trial, his heart ached for two of the young men, who were obviously younger than the others. Steven knew the parents of these two. One of the two, Gilbert Collins, only fifteen years old, was from a broken home and lived with his mother. The other, Calvin Keller was sixteen years old, and was the son of two parents, both of whom had full-time jobs, and sadly had little time for their son. Steven felt sure that the boys had been victims of choosing bad companions. He recalled his father's advice to him, "Don't be deceived; bad companions corrupt good morals."

Steven went and talked to the parents. His original impression only deepened. He felt these were good kids, who with proper adult encouragement and guidance would not have gotten involved in the mischief that brought them into court. He could not really blame the parents because he saw that in difficult circumstances they were doing the best they could, but sadly had let some parental responsibilities slip.

Steven then talked to the judge who was hearing the case and would pronounce sentence on the young men. He shared his concern, and the judge concurred with Steven's analysis of the kids; he believed four of the young men needed to be incarcerated in the juvenile offender facility of the county. However, he also felt concern for the two youngest of the six, and said he was disposed to assign them to community service.

Steven immediately volunteered to be responsible for Gil and Cal if the judge would assign them to him. He said he knew of several projects in the city where two such young men could well be used. The judge immediately thanked Steven for his offer. When time

COMPASSION AND COURAGE

for sentencing came, the judge sentenced four of the young men to time in the Juvenile Detention Center, but sentenced Gil and Cal to one hundred hours each of community service under Steven's supervision.

Steven assigned Gil and Cal to work with the service club that had volunteered to maintain the expanding city park. One afternoon as he wrapped up his work in the city manager's office, Steven decided to go over to the park and see how things were going with Gil, Cal and the volunteers who were working there. As he arrived, they were just finishing up trimming some bushes. Steven told the volunteers they could go home, and he would help Gil and Cal take the tools they had been using to the storage shed. As the three of them were closing the shed, they saw two young men approaching them from the parking lot. As the two strode toward them, it could be seen that one of them had a chain and the other a baseball bat. Cal exclaimed, with obvious fear in his voice, "It's Crusher and Masher." Even though they wore ski masks, Cal recognized them as two of the muscle men in the gang Gil and Cal had formerly been in. He shouted, "We'd better get out of here Gil," and ran toward the woods where hiking trails wound through the wilderness part of the park. However, Gil stood beside Steven, who had taken a firm stand facing the approaching hoodlums. The two stood face to face with Steven Morganton and Gil. One of them was swinging the chain like a pendulum, and the other softly striking the palm of one hand with the bat, grasping it, releasing it, and then striking it again. They said, "We don't have any bone to pick with you, "Mr. City Guy," but Gil and his buddy who just ran into the woods seem to have forgotten that no one leaves the "Scorchers." If you'll just let Gil come with us now, no one will get hurt. But if he doesn't come, both of you are in for some serious hurt. Steven felt a quiver of fear run through his entire being. Yet, summoning up every ounce of courage within him he was able to respond in a voice so strong and convincing that he himself was surprised, "Gil is not going anywhere, and you are just asking for more trouble for yourselves." The two kept up their slow swinging of the chain and the rhythmic soft pounding of the bat into the palm of his hand.

The one with the bat shook it in the face of Gil and said, "You'd better come with us and forget this city guy, or you're going to be sorry you don't."

CRACK.! The sound echoed through the park. The one they called Crusher shouted, "Where did that come from? Who has a gun around here?" Masher said, "Calm down, Crusher. No one has a gun." Crusher said, "Look back in the woods. I think I see a rifle barrel where that tree divides into two trunks." Then they heard the voice of Cal, "Masher and Crusher, you guys get out of here. Next time it won't be just a warning shot."

Crusher and Masher started to back away slowly. Then they heard the piercing sound of a police car siren and turned and their pace became a full speed sprint toward the car they had left in the parking lot. The police car came to a screeching stop in the parking lot, and two policeman stepped out. Steven shouted, "Officers, stop those men!" The officers drew their side arms, arrested the men, put handcuffs on them, and put them in the police car to take them to the station for questioning. Steven and Gil came to the officers, and Steven asked them why they were coming to the park with their siren blasting. Pointing to a nearby house they said, "We received a call from a neighbor that she heard what she believed to be a gun shot from the park. As we pulled in, we saw these two men running toward their car, and when you yelled for us to stop them, we did. We'll take them to the station, and find out what this is all about."

COMPASSION AND COURAGE

Steven told them, "I'll come right down to the station and tell you about their threats to us, but first I need to go see where Cal has gone."

As Steven and Gil started back through the park toward the woods on the other side, they saw Cal coming from the hiking trail through the woods. Gil said, "Cal, you're some friend, taking off and running when you saw Masher and Crusher coming." "Follow me," Cal said, "I want to show you something."

As they were walking through the park toward the trail that led into the woods, Cal asked, "Remember the cabin that is being built in the woods?" "We sure do," responded Steven. It was one of the projects for upgrading and expanding the park. In keeping with Steven's suggestion, the city had decided to build a cabin along the hiking trail which would be rented out as a week-end or vacation cabin. Rockview was in a rather scenic part of the state with gently rolling hills, and three lakes in the area. The town was becoming popular as a quiet retreat for people who wanted to get away for relaxation and renewal. Steven's brother, Philip, had provided all the architectural drawings for the cabins at no cost to the city. The first cabin was a bit of an experiment, and if it proved feasible, and showed a profit, or even just paid for itself, the city was planning to build several more. This first cabin had been under construction for a few weeks.

Cal went on: "I remember that a construction crew was working on that cabin. When I saw Crusher and Masher coming, I knew we were in trouble. I ran back to the woods to ask the construction crew if they would come to give us some help against those guys. When I got there, the crew had left for the day."

Cal pointed to a three quarter inch diameter piece of water pipe, with about five inches of its length showing in the crotch of the double-trunk tree. "I placed that pipe there, hoping that a few inches protruding toward where you were standing might look like a rifle barrel. Now listen to this" Cal went on. "I found this plank" he picked up a one by eight board about six feet long "lying here on the concrete. Listen to this." Cal lifted one end of the board about three feet from the ground, leaving the other end resting on the concrete. Then he placed one foot in about the middle of the board, and pushed down with all his might, pushing the board as hard as he could forcing it down to the concrete. CRACK! The impact of the board against concrete sounded like a gun shot.

"Wow," said Steven. "That was sure clever of you. And it worked. You not only saved us from what would have been a severe beating, but you helped apprehend two of the hoodlums who were a part of the gang you used to run with."

Steven took Gil and Cal with him as he drove to the police station. On the way they stopped at the house the officer had pointed out from which the call had come reporting what sounded like a gun shot to tell them what had taken place, and to assure them that the matter was taken care of, and that things were safe now. The lady of the house said she had been working in her yard when she heard the sound, and had hurried into the house to call the police. "You did exactly the right thing," Steven told the lady, "and you have helped apprehend a couple of renegades who needed to be caught."

When they arrived at the police station, the officers had already begun an interrogation of "Masher" and "Crusher." Disarmed of their baseball bat and chain and without the ski masks they were not nearly so tough. The information they gave the police would result in stopping much of the gang activity that had plagued the area.

Steven recounted all that had happened; the threats of the two the police had in custody and the clever acts of Cal that stopped the beating. The officers complimented Cal on his quick thinking and clever acts. Then Steven said, "I'm am learning more and more the truth my father taught me; that all things work together for those living in keeping with God's purpose. Consider this: that pipe and board were laying right where Cal quickly saw them, his quick thinking brought to mind a plan that resulted in those ruffians not beating us, the woman was working in her yard and heard the clap of that board against the concrete that sounded like a gunshot and called the police, your patrol car was in the immediate neighborhood. Now we can dismiss all those as coincidences, and maybe they were, but it seems to me there must have been something, or Someone, who was involved in all those 'coincidences' and somehow was working them together." "You could well be right," one of the officers commented, "You could well be right."

As they were walking from the police station to drive Gil and Cal home, Steven placed his arms over the boys' shoulders and said, "I'm proud of you guys. This was an exciting afternoon, wasn't it?" How do you feel about the whole thing?"

Cal answered with a big grin. "It feels great! I never knew it could be so satisfying to be on the right side of the law."

Under Steven's management, it had been a great year for the city of Rockview. At the end of the year, the city declared Steven Morganton to be "Man of the Year," and the city council voted him a ten percent raise.

Several weeks later Steven said to Kim one evening. "Honey, you have been a real trouper. You supported me in my decision to leave the real estate development company, and you have been absolutely magnificent in working in our vegetable garden, managing the kids and the produce stand. You have turned it into a profitable business.

However, you have been working too hard, and I want to make it easier for you."

"And how do you plan to do that, Mr. City Manager?" she asked with that near giggle in her voice.

"We are doing well with the produce stand, and I've decide to plow three more acres and expand the garden. I thought we might also build a hen house and sell eggs with our produce. The horses and the chickens would provide fertilizer for the garden. We will then have ten acres of garden, five acres where we pasture our two horses, and still have three acres here where the house and the pool are located."

"That sounds brilliant, Mr. Entrepreneur. But pray tell me how will that make things easier for me. It sounds like a lot MORE work."

Steven answered, "I'd like to hire Gil and Cal to work for us part time. During the rest of the school year they could work after school hours, and then when summer comes and there is more work in the garden, we could use them for more hours each week."

"I like the idea, Honey," Kim said, "but I'm concerned what it might mean to Gil and Cal with their school work. They haven't made the best grades, you know."

"You're right," was Steven's response. "They haven't in the past, but I've talked with their teachers and they've told me their grades have improved since getting away from those gangs they were running with. Besides, I have a plan where we might help them with some tutoring. Cal needs some help with English, and Gil could use some help with Math."

Evenings at the Steven Morganton house became most interesting. Gil and Cal would come after school and work for a couple or hours, then they would sit with Steven and Kim while Kim helped Cal with English, and Steven tutored Gil in math. Sometimes the boys would stay and have supper with the Morganton's. When summer came the work in the garden was often followed by a dip in the pool, and then a cookout. About one evening a week Cal's parents and Gil's mother would join them. A deep friendship developed among these families. The following school year both Cal and Gil's grades improved markedly.

THE FINAL GLORY

For Robert and Karen Morganton life went on with the ecstasies and agonies common to the human sojourn. Their agony at the time of Steven's days of doubt and waywardness were displaced by the ecstasy they experienced by his return to faith and his fruitful service to God and the community. They experienced the joy of watching Phillip, Ruth, Esther, Ramón and Ramona mature into responsible and productive adults and parents. They often knew the ecstasy of seeing marriages mended and saved in the lives of those whom they counseled. They knew the joy of seeing wandering, helpless lost people come to know Christ and experience the joy that is to be found in Him. However, they also knew the agony of seeing people whom they loved and to whom they had spent hours seeking to lead them to Christ reject their witness and turn away from God. They felt deep pain each time a husband and wife, in spite of all the counsel they could give them, would divorce and break up a home. Even more painful was the agony of seeing brothers and sisters in Christ, members of the church they served, fall away and turn from Christ and His kingdom. Through the times of agony they prayed hard and sought God's guidance and comfort, and through the times of ecstasy they praised God for His goodness and blessings.

Through the years of his ministry the Rockview church continued to grow. There were times when it would plateau for a while, and even decline in attendance, but these were short, and would be followed by a time of renewed vigor and growth.

When Bob reached sixty-five years of age, he submitted his resignation to the elders of the Rockview congregation. However, by a unanimous vote they refused this resignation, and urged him to continue to minister with the church. He agreed to stay on for a while. When he was seventy years old he began to share much of the preaching ministry with Andrew Matson, the Family Life Minister. It became obvious that brother Matson was well qualified, and would serve well as the preaching minister of the church. When he was seventy-two years old, Bob once again submitted his resignation with the suggestion that Andrew Matson become the preaching minister, and a search be made for another Family Life Minister. After much prayer and many expressions of appreciation for the work Bob Morganton had done through the years, his suggestion was taken. The transition went smoothly, as it had when Bob first became their minister. For the next several years Bob continued to live in Rockview, but did considerable preaching as a supply minister or for conferences, evangelistic meetings and various rallies in the area. He remained strong, healthy and vigorous until late in his seventies.

Then the cancer struck. When diagnosed Bob was told that this was a very aggressive cancer for which there was no cure, and that he only had a few months to live.

Those months were filled with many hours, and sometimes days, of precious times with his family. This family, including Bob and Karen's natural children, Ramón and Ramona and their children, had now grown to a total of twenty six people. They came to visit Bob and Karen as often as they could, and stayed as long as possible. There were days when Bob was extremely weak, barely coherent, and slept most of the time. There were other days when he was alert and lucid and immensely enjoyed their company. Knowing of Bob's limited time, these were days filled with some sadness, but with many hours of precious memories, some joyful reminiscing and a lot of laughter. Bob had lived well, and was prepared to die well.

When the time came that it was obvious that death would come in a matter of a few days. Bob was moved to a suite in the hospital that had been built especially for those in the last days of life. The Rockview congregation where Bob had ministered for decades had originated the idea of such a facility, and had been a major contributor to it. Other congregations and civic organizations had contributed to its construction and maintenance. With such support it was made available for families with loved ones in their final days for about the cost of ordinary hospital rooms. It consisted of a large room for the patient, with several chairs and other furniture where several people could visit at the same time. Adjacent to it was another room with a bed where family members could stay around the clock. It had been dubbed the "Final Farewell" suite. The Rockview church told the Morganton family that they had secured and paid for this suite for Bob's final days. It was here that Bob spent the last week of his life on this earth.

During that last week there was a constant stream of visitors for Bob. If he were sleeping, or did not seem well enough to have company they would only inquire about him, express their concern and leave. At other times he was able to converse with those who came.

Karen stayed with Bob nearly around the clock, sleeping in the adjacent room and leaving only to eat and go home and bath and change clothes. Phillip, Ruth and Esther and Steven came by for a visit every day.

One day Steven stood by Bob's bedside, took his hand and said, "Dad, I must apologize to you for the things I said when Susan was so sick." "Bob interrupted. "Son, no apology is necessary." "Yes it is," Steven replied. "I must tell you how wrong I was, and how ashamed I am of it, and how right you were. I was hurting because of the death of our first child, was resentful and blamed God because Bradley had Downs Syndrome, and was sure Susan was about to die. But God mercifully spared Susan's life, and you know what a normal and precious child she is. And Bradley, what a blessing he has been. He has such a gentle and kind spirit. He finds his greatest joy in doing something to help someone. We have learned so many things from him. During the times when he was so dependent upon us we learned how dependent we are upon our Heavenly Father, and how patient He must be with us. At times when Bradley accomplished things on his own, and you know those have been numerous and significant, we felt a deep pride in him. It made us realize how God must rejoice in the good things we do, in spite of our unworthiness and weakness. Yes, Bradley has been a rich blessing to us in many ways. And just four years ago, past the time when most men become fathers, God blessed Kim and me with the birth of Jacob. Dad, your life has demonstrated it, and your teaching has made me realize that to those who love God and are called according to His purpose, all things truly do work out for good. Thank you for that. I only hope that I can make that conviction evident in my life to even half the degree you did, and that I will be able to pass such a conviction on to my children."

When it was obvious that Bob was in his final hours, all the children were summoned and came to the Final Farewell suite. Bob was sleeping deeply when they arrived, but in a few moments rallied, and became surprisingly alert and lucid. Through a weak voice he was able to talk with his family. He told all of them how much he loved them and how proud he was of every one of them. One by one, he took each one of his sons and daughters by the hand, and much like Jacob of the Bible, when he was dying, he had words of encouragement which he spoke to each one of his children individually. He asked each one of them about their children, and smiled weakly as they told him about his grandchildren.

Steven was the last, and Bob's question was about Jacob, his four year old. Steven answered, "Jacob is doing fine, and Dad, he's the grandchild whose going to carry on your legacy. I'm certain he's going to be a preacher." Bob asked, "How can you be so sure when he's only four years old that he's going to be a preacher?"

Steven answered, "He thinks he knows everything, and he can't stop talking."

Just outside the "Final Farewell" unit where some of the staff were waiting and listening the response was much like that in the courtroom when Bob was sentenced to prison. They commented to each other, "Have you ever heard laughter come from the room of someone on the brink of death?" "Never" they said one to another. "I in all my experience have not seen anyone approach death with such peace and contentment."

After his words with each of his children individually, they all joined hands around the bed, and Phillip worded a prayer of thanksgiving for the life his father had lived, and asked the Lord's presence in a powerful way in these final moments. As he concluded, Bob said, "and remember, all things work... (now the whole family joined him in unison as they said) "together for those who love God, those who are called according to His purpose." Finally, Bob took Karen by the hand. She bent over him, told him she loved him with all her heart. He answered "Karen, I'm sure you know how much

I love you. How blessed I am. When I was alone and seeking to rebuild my life after years in prison, God brought you into my life. He united us in ministry, and then in marriage. You have made my life rich and full. You gave me four beautiful children, and joined me in the adoption of two other precious souls. You have stood with me in good and difficult times. Never could anyone expect a better wife and helpmeet."

Bob's voice had been weakening as he spoke, and was now only a whisper. His eyes closed, and he seemed to draw a deep breath. Then he opened his eyes, gave a slight tug on Karen's hand, and she brought her lips to his. He gave her a gentle kiss, and said, "Goodnight, my darling. I'll see you in the morning."

Then his eyes closed, his breathing stopped, and his heartbeat ceased.

Again the personnel in the Final Farewell suite were astounded. From Bob's room came the words, not with the volume with which they were usually sung, but with a rich blend and beautiful harmony came the song: "FOR THE LORD GOD OMNIPOTENT REIGNETH. HALLELUJAH." (14)

The End
and the beginning

END NOTES

1. This scenario parallels the real life event of Mr. and Mrs. Ollie Carlock, their son John and Doctors Holmes and Kenyon at the South Miami, Florida hospital.

2. This event has its real life counterpart in the case of Dennis Marshall. The hospital was Florida Hospital near Orlando, Florida. The real life doctors were Dr. George Swarez-Cavelier, surgeon, Dr. Baiju, Cardiologist, Andros Pelaez, pulmonary hypertension technician, and Cynthia Paulikas, nurse practitioner in Florida, and Dr. Nick Kim, University of California, in San Diego.

3. I Samuel 1:8

4. See Malachi 2:14-1

5. This story was told to the author by Mary Bolen, about two of her daughters, the author's granddaughters.

6. Ibid.

7. Philippians 4:6,7

8. See Gen. 45:5

END NOTES

9. *Philippians 1:12*

10. *Such Communion Table Baptisteries are supplied to prisons by American Rehabilitation Ministries.*

11. *American Rehabilitation Ministries also supplies such Bible study courses for prisoners.*

12. *This incident has it's real life counterpart when the author's brother, Clayton Marshall fell from a scaffold while working on a sign in Opa Locka, Florida advertising Renuart, Bailey, Cheely lumber company in 1967.*

13. *The incident of Susan's meningitis and recovery had its real life counterpart when the author's son was stricken in 1966 at the age of 8 months. He was in Children's Variety Hospital in Miami, Florida for several days. A concerted participation in prayer was orchestrated from Florida to Michigan.*

14. *From the "Hallelujah" chorus of Handel's Messiah.*

CPSIA information can be obtained
at www.ICGtesting.com
Printed in the USA
FSOW03n0548170118
42958FS